I heard it again—the sound of someone walking stealthily toward me in the sand. I rolled on my belly, gathered my legs beneath me and dived at an indistinct figure five feet away. We went down. There was a muffled sound of surprise. My hand slid along a smooth curved thigh, touched rounded breasts and full nipples. I was holding a woman as naked as I was, and holding her damned tight, the weight of my body pinning her to the sand. I backed away from her fast and she sat up. She cried out again, reached toward her breasts with protective hands.

"I'm sorry," I said. "You shouldn't have come up behind me like that."

"It's...all right," she said in a strained voice. "I'm sorry I...startled you." Her hands came away from her breasts slowly and dropped to her knees. She sat very still, apparently looking toward me. I hadn't held her long, but long enough for her to be perfectly aware I wasn't dressed either. Not that it made any difference, in the dark.

"Who are you?" I said.

"I'm Diane. You...must be Pete Mallory."

"That's right. How did you know?"

"Macy's talked about you. He brought you here to find the person who's going to kill him."

"Yes."

She was silent for a moment. Then she stretched, rising to her toes, and relaxed. Her voice was calm again.

"Macy will tell you about me," she said. "I'm supposed to be a little bit crazy."

"Are you?"

She laughed girlishly. "I suppose so. I suppose I am..."

Baby MOLL

by John Farris

WRITING AS 'STEVE BRACKEEN'

A HARD CASE CRIME NOVEL

A HARD CASE CRIME BOOK
(HCC-046)
August 2008

Published by

Dorchester Publishing Co., Inc.
200 Madison Avenue
New York, NY 10016

in collaboration with Winterfall LLC

*This book is a work of fiction. Names, characters, places, and
incidents either are the products of the author's imagination or
are used fictitiously, and any resemblance to actual events or
persons, living or dead, is entirely coincidental.*

ISBN 0-8439-5964-9
ISBN-13 978-0-8439-5964-2

Cover design by Cooley Design Lab

Typeset by Swordsmith Productions

The name "Hard Case Crime" and the Hard Case Crime logo
are trademarks of Winterfall LLC. Hard Case Crime books are
selected and edited by Charles Ardai.

Printed in the United States of America

Visit us on the web at www.HardCaseCrime.com

BABY MOLL

Chapter One

We had fun that day, the day Rudy Mask turned up in Orange Bay to reweave the net that held me to the past. In the morning Elaine and I took the boat through the calm waters of the pass and hunted south along the coast for snook, and, later, when the chest was full, for a beach and growth of trees where we could rest and swim.

I decided on a curved narrow piece of island three or four hundred yards from the shoreline, and edged the boat into the beach. Elaine slipped over the side into shallow water to guide the keel against the sand.

"Catch me," I said, then jumped over the side, splashing water on her swimsuit.

"Pete!" she wailed.

"So what?" I chided. "That's what it's for, isn't it? To get wet?"

She backed away and waded indignantly out of the water. I followed with towels and the basket of lunch. She was good to watch. A tall girl with long legs, a smooth straight walk. She wore a blue bathing suit, cut high at the firm thighs, fitting snugly over the slender curve of waist and small breasts. Made to run, quick and laughing, along the beaches, to lie in the sun that nourished her slender strength. I had found her on a beach, and had known the ache of wanting something so much that the long months of waiting were almost unendurable.

I spread the beach towels when Elaine indicated a desirable spot. "We eat?" I said.

She turned her face to me. "Not yet." She took off her seaman's cap, harshly white against the glistening black of her hair, flipped at her bangs with a knuckle. Her lips formed the slanted grin I liked. "You stink of fish, mister. Bathe yourself."

"You come too."

"No. I—"

I took her wrist. "Come on."

"Pete, I don't—" She brought the edge of her wrist up against my thumb, breaking the hold. "Don't go cave man on me. I really don't want to swim—"

I beat on my chest, Tarzan fashion, and made a grab for her. She choked back laughter, squirmed out of reach. I chased her toward the water, running full tilt. She stopped suddenly, ducked, stuck out a foot. I tumbled into the water, came up gasping.

"You've got sand in your hair now." She grinned, panting. "Better wash it out as long as you're in there."

I went into the water, pushed deep into the coolness, swam until my lungs were hot and bursting. Then I broke surface and took air, blinking the sting of salt from my eyes. The sun was a hot flare lashing at my face. The sky was a blue shield that threw back the heat and softened the glare. There was a whisper of breeze. I swam easily and slowly back to the beach. My arms made slow rippling splashes, the only sound other than the far laughter of the girl as she ran through shallow white water, kicking up spray to sparkle in the sunlight. It was a good morning. It would be a good afternoon, too. Then the sun would deepen and grow large behind the fringe of trees on the shore and it would be time to go home. I felt the old thin taste of fear rising in my throat. There had been too many good days. Soon maybe the luck would begin to tarnish.

I waded to shore and took Elaine by the hand. She walked beside me, breathing deeply, her eyes gleaming. We had our lunch, then stretched out on the beach towels. I took lotion and rubbed her shoulders and back. She stretched, the long muscles in her legs tight, then relaxed. After a few seconds she looked at me with one eye and smiled like a little girl who doesn't quite know how to pick up a kitten. She cupped a hand behind my head and brought my face to hers, kissed me. It started gently and became fierce and demanding. I lay down beside her. I touched an ear and the tip of her nose and traced the fine lips with the tip of my finger, tracing that crazy smile which makes me feel warm in a place deep inside that I once thought was forever scarred.

"Talky today, aren't you?" she said lazily, her eyes smiling.

"Sometimes words are just a nuisance."

She closed her eyes for a moment. Her hand touched my shoulder, slipped down my arm. Her fingers closed around my wrist, worried the hand gently. "Yes," she said. "Such a man. Such a big man for me. Such a big man to love. How I love you, Pete." The eyes opened and she looked at me somberly. "You're not worried about something, are you?"

I tried not to let my smile fade. "What would I have to worry about? I own my own business and I'm about to marry the most beautiful girl in the state. Even her old man is beginning to like me. Me worry?"

"Don't try to kid—" she warned, but I stopped her with a kiss. I overdid it a little because I wanted to shut off whatever she was thinking about me. She knew me too well to distrust any of her intuitions.

I felt her body stiffen. "Hey," she said, "you...trying to start something?"

"Yes." I kissed her again, and she responded readily.

But she said firmly, "No, Pete."

"We're going to be married."

"We're not married yet."

"All we haven't had is the ceremony."

"But we really shouldn't...that was just...you're so damn persuasive."

"And I love you."

She sighed, surrendering. "I guess it wouldn't make—"

I worked the top of her suit down from her breasts.

"Oh, Pete," she said comfortably, and helped me with the suit.

Afterwards she slept and I sat beside her, my skin very white where the swim trunks had been, and watched the small swell of waves on the beach, and tried not to think. But I had to look at her and wonder if her love could be strong enough, if it really would make no difference to her should I have to tell her where I came from, and what I was. There was no way to know. Maybe she loved me enough and could take that kind of shock. She was a pretty solid girl, unspoiled by the effects of wealth and social prestige that were hers and her family's. But they, the proud Arnells, wouldn't get over it. And they would take her away from me. One way or another, they'd do it.

After an hour, she stirred behind me, and I saw one

foot lift as she stretched. Then she sat up and put her face against my back, her arms around me.

"You love me, Pete." It wasn't a question.

"You know that."

She was silent. The arms tightened about me, then relaxed. I sat very still, feeling the tips of her small breasts against my back as she breathed. I pushed the heel of my hand against my stiff-cropped hedge of hair, brushed loose a few grains of sand.

"Is there something you want to tell me, Pete?" she asked.

"No. Why?"

She began to rock back and forth gently, rocking me with her.

"When we left the store this morning, there was a custard-colored Pontiac coming down the street. Do you remember? It came slow at first, and the driver was looking at us. Then it speeded up. You were holding my hand so tight it hurt. When I glanced at you, for a second or two, the look in your eyes frightened me. Did you recognize the driver, or something?"

I looked incredulously at her. "No. Of course not. You been having bad dreams?"

She touched her lips to my back once, then stood up and straightened out the swimsuit, put it on thoughtfully.

"No. No, I haven't had any bad dreams. Have you?"

I picked up my own suit and squirmed into it. It was about three; time to leave soon.

Her eyebrows drew together as she fitted the elastic top over her breasts. There was a funny look in her eyes, as if she were remembering being hurt a long time ago and didn't like thinking about it.

"Pete," she said in a flat voice, "what did you do before you came to Orange Bay?"

"Oh, I was in the Army for a while. Then I worked down in Castile for an insurance company. When I got bored with it I came North and opened up the sports shop. I thought I'd rather fish when I felt like it than adjust claims. Life story. You know all that. Then I met you. My life really started then."

"I don't believe you ever told me the name of the insurance company you worked for."

I frowned, not liking all the questions. "Bay State Mutual. Why? Is it important?"

"No. I guess not."

"Look, Elaine. I'm fine today. A little moody, possibly. Those feelings come and go. Don't start worrying about me."

She brushed at her bangs with the back of one hand. Her smile was quick but uncertain. "I'm sorry, darling."

"I guess it's time for us to get out of here," I said.

"Yes." She turned her head to look at the angle of the sun. "It was a nice day," she said. "I had fun today." She held my hand tightly. "I wish…it wouldn't end."

"There'll be other good days," I said. "Lots of good days." I wasn't thinking that. I was thinking that maybe the good days were over for a while. And I was afraid she'd know, so I turned away from her and began to gather up the beach towels.

We walked to the water and I helped Elaine over the side into the boat, shoved off from the beach. Once at the wheel I headed into the sun. Elaine leaned against me, her head on my shoulder. Her eyes were closed. The boat cut a rough path through the darkening water. She hummed to herself, and I could barely hear the sound of it above the noise of the big motor. It was a strange lonesome tune that no one had ever hummed before but everyone had heard it at some time, sounding clear above the low beat of fear in their hearts.

Chapter Two

Elaine was in better spirits by the time we arrived at her home. I unloaded the car, carried the beach towels and picnic basket to the big front porch of the Arnell house, overlooking the bay.

"Don't forget the concert tonight," she reminded me. "You've got only an hour to get ready."

I kissed her cheek lightly. "I'll go over to the store now and change. Clean the fish in the morning."

I drove away from the house and headed crosstown. On the way I passed through the neighborhood where our house had recently been completed. It was dark now, waiting for Mrs. Mallory to bring light and warmth to the rooms. Soon. My breath caught a little at the thought. It had been a damned long time. But she had been worth waiting for.

My store was south on the highway, convenient for both the fresh-water fisherman of the backcountry canals and the angler who favors the tide flats and open sea.

I parked in front of the small building and paused under the pulsing neon sign that identified the place as *The Angler's Shop* to find the doorkey. Locating in this section had cost me practically all my savings, but in two years the investment had paid off in a new house.

Thinking about this, I looked self-consciously down the street, but there were no cars parked nearby. My only company was two teen-age girls in Bermuda shorts standing in front of a theater half a block away. I grimaced at my momentary nervousness and unlocked the door. I put away a couple of lures I had been experimenting with that morning and hunted up an ice chest. While I was getting it from a shelf behind the display case, the door opened. It didn't close right away, and I had the feeling that someone held it open and watched me. Sweat rolled down my cheek. It was hot in the store without the air conditioner on. There was a loaded .38 revolver in a holster beneath the cash register, but it was ten steps away. I could feel the muscles of my back tightening. I tried not to think about the gun.

"You went fishing today," he said. "I couldn't find you."

I took the ice chest from the shelf, straightened up and turned around, setting the chest carefully on the glass top of the display case. A drop of perspiration fell from my chin, splashing on the glass. I was conscious of my heart beating too fast.

"You ever been shot, Rudy?" I said harshly.

He was a stocky man, with too much weight on his bones now. He wore a wrinkled light-blue cord suit, a tired gray hat pushed back on his head. His hair was graying, oiled, long around the ears, thinning on top. He watched me steadily, wearily, from behind a large pair of glasses, the clear plastic frames yellowed by the sun. There was a crack at the corner of one lens.

His lips stretched wide in a humorless smile. "Lots of times."

"You know better than to come on me like that. You might have picked up another one."

A brown insect with buzzing wings whirled in the door, hovered near his ear, soared away. He chewed steadily on the wood end of a match. "You wasn't nowhere near a gun," he said, then added defensively, as if he hadn't considered the possibility before, "and I was as close as my hip pocket."

"Finish coming in," I told him, "and shut the door." I walked around the display case and turned on the air conditioner at the back of the store.

Rudy Mask sat in a chair and looked curiously about the store, sighed as the cold air from the big Carrier unit reached him. "So this is what you bought with Macy's money," he said.

I stood watching him. "Money I earned, Rudy," I said.

He nodded, taking in the stuffed sailfish, the racks of slender rods. He knew nothing about fishing, cared less. He was an old hoodlum, an aging tough guy, his body scarred from knives and an occasional healed bullet wound. Not many. You don't take many and keep walking around. His face and ears were worn and lined from the back alley poundings, the careless brawls in dives in every kind of town. His eyes had seen too many women, in brothels, in stinking chicken coops when things were bad, in magnificent apartments that smelled of strange flowers and perfume and the sweet flesh of hundred-dollar girls when things were fabulously good. His fingers had held too much whisky, and they weren't steady.

It had been six and a half years since I had seen him, and he didn't belong here. I didn't want to see him now. I had left his kind of life one day when the stink of it had clutched at my stomach and made sleep impossible.

In the last months I had gradually forgotten there was always a loaded gun pointed at my head wherever I went. Rudy was a reminder that the trigger could be pulled at any time.

"What are you doing in Orange Bay?" I asked him.

"Macy wants you." He took the chewed match from his mouth, glanced at it, tossed it on the floor. He looked for another in his coat pocket. "Somebody's going to kill him," he said, and coughed. Then it was quiet in the store, except for the air conditioner.

"Is that supposed to make me unhappy?" I said.

"Well, Jesus!" Rudy said, surprised.

"Who's trying to kill him and why would I be interested?" I said, impatient to know what he was getting at.

He shook his head. "Macy doesn't know. It's not a Syndicate order."

"What *does* he know?"

Rudy shifted his weight in the chair. "You remember the old gang, Macy's first gang, back in the thirties? I started with Macy then, after I drifted out of Kansas City. There were four others besides me, Pete. Clemente and Porter and Tin Ear and Lundquist. Did Macy ever tell you what racket we had then?"

"Shakedown. Protection."

"It was sweet. We lined up whole neighborhoods. Once in a while a customer wouldn't buy. We ran into a tailor like that. He had a scrubby little shop and lived upstairs with fat mamma and two-three kiddies. Little old guy with a bent back and thick glasses. I remember him kinda well. He didn't need the protection. His place burned one night. It was tough. So quick he didn't have time to get himself and fat mamma and the kiddies out. We lost a client, but the other merchants on the block came through in a hurry."

"I never heard about it," I said grimly.

"Macy's been hearing about it lately—in the last three years. Every time one of the old gang was knocked off, he got a clipping in the mail, an old yellow newspaper clipping about the fire that burned the tailor and his family. Along with another story about how each one of the boys got it. Porter was the first. In an alley in Hammond, Indiana, about three years ago. Ripped apart with a big knife. There was maybe a couple of paragraphs in the local paper. Nobody would have known about it, except Macy got the story a few days later, cut from the paper. And the first clipping about the fire."

"Who else is dead?"

Rudy slicked back his dirty hair, pressed a hand against his abdomen. "Stomach's kind of wacky lately," he explained apologetically. He took a couple of hard breaths. "Clemente went back to Cuba after the war. I think it was about seven months after Porter was killed that Macy got the story about Clemente. In Spanish, yet. His woman found him hung upside down in some Havana crib, slit open from throat to groin."

"Another clipping about the fire with this newspaper story?"

"Right…Let's see. It was Tin Ear next. New Orleans, this time. Throat cut and belly opened. About a year after Clemente. Three weeks ago Lundquist was knifed in an old folks' home outside of Tampa."

"Any message with these clippings? Some kind of threat?"

"Hell, no. It's clear enough, ain't it?"

"Yeah. Macy's getting shook about all this?"

"Not too much. But he wants to get this thing off his back. He's got other problems. He wants you to find the guy with the knife who's sending him these newspaper stories."

"How about you, Rudy?" I said. "You getting worried?"

He rubbed the back of his hand across his lumpy chin. His eyes weren't happy. He was beginning to look like an old man. "The guy sticks with it," he said, his voice rasping. "It takes a lot of patience to hunt down men like he does."

"And a lot of hate to use a knife like that."

"Yeah," Rudy said. He squirmed in the chair.

I packed the ice chest with ice from the refrigerator, put the fish inside. It was time for me to pick Elaine up. She would begin to wonder what was keeping me. I thought of the menace of Rudy Mask, and Macy Barr, who should have been untouchable, but was feeling the pressure from a slow and patient killer. I wondered if I was going to be able to say no to Macy again and get away with it.

Without looking at Rudy I said, "Tell Macy to get another boy. I made a clean break. I want it to stay clean."

Rudy was silent.

"If he told you to bring me whether I wanted to come or not, forget that too," I told him.

"He didn't figure you'd come back because you love him so much," Rudy said. "So he wanted me to remind you of something. About what a nice girl you're engaged to."

I turned, my jaw tight with rage. Rudy wasn't gloating. He looked at me soberly. "He wouldn't hurt your girl," Rudy said. "He wouldn't have somebody brought in to hurt her and leave her in an alley without her clothes like he's done to others. He just said he'd take a letter you wrote a long time ago and wrap it up and send it to her so she could read it." He was watching me closely. He must have seen what happened to my eyes, because he grunted, satisfied, and walked away, poking his bad teeth with the end of a match.

No, Macy wouldn't hurt Elaine. Not in the old manner, breaking bones and faces. Once in a while this was the best way, the only way to make sure a warning was obeyed, to maintain control of the uncertain human element in a sprawling illicit operation. But through the years Macy had learned better and safer ways of control: how to bring a man to his knees through the gentle pressure of his own mistakes; how to hit a man through others close to him so that it is more painful than any beating.

The letter would tell Elaine what I had never told her: about a wife named Jean, whose home for five years had been an institution in New York State until in a lucid moment some time ago she had slashed herself and bled to death. It would be the beginning of ruin. Maybe Elaine could take it. But if her mother and father found out… They weren't sure of me, anyway. And if they should start looking into my past, I was through.

Rudy stood near the front window watching the cars go by in the street, jingling change in his pocket. I heard the telephone and picked up the receiver without thinking about it.

"Pete?" Elaine said cheerfully. "You break your leg or something?"

"I was just leaving," I said thickly. "Be right over."

"Nothing wrong, is there?"

"No. Of course not. See you in a little while."

I put the receiver down. Rudy yawned. "We'll have to get moving. Macy was expecting us today."

"You bastard," I said.

"I'm sorry, Pete," he said, sounding as if he really meant it.

Chapter Three

Elaine answered the door when I rang the bell. She was wearing a pastry-pink semiformal dress and the edges of her short black hair sparkled. A welcoming smile faded when she saw me.

"Pete, you're not dressed!"

I went on inside. "Anyone else home?"

She frowned as if she were beginning to get angry with me. "No. Mother and Dad left ten minutes ago. Why—"

I couldn't look at her. "I'm going away for a few days, Elaine. I have to leave tonight."

She didn't get it right away. She stood silently looking at me as if I were out of my mind.

"What are you talking about, Pete?" Her voice was high.

It was getting worse by the second. I tried not to yell at her because of the hurt I was feeling. "I just said I have to go away. That's all. I'll be back in a few days."

"Oh." Her hands brushed at the crisp ruffles on her dress. "It's kind of sudden, isn't it? Where are you going that you have to leave in such a hurry?"

"To the south. It's—business. I didn't know about it until a few minutes ago."

She put a hand to her cheek. Her mouth turned down at the corners. "Nice of you to come by and tell me about it."

"Damn it, Elaine, don't—"

She took two quick steps and put her arms around

me. Her eyes were frightened. "Pete, what is it? You're acting—I never saw you like this. Are you in some kind of trouble? Is that—Oh, Pete, what's the matter?"

"Does anything have to be the matter? I'm just going to Castile for a few days."

"Tell me why," she whispered. "You can do that."

I held her. "No. I—It's not imp—"

She broke away from me, looked at me, her eyes full of rage and hurt. "You don't really love me so much after all, do you?"

"There are some things it's better for you not to—"

"*What* things? What are you talking about? This morning that car—now you suddenly have to leave town—" Her voice broke. "All right, leave. Go ahead and leave, Pete. But don't come back. Ever. Not until you think I'm important enough in your life to help you when you need help."

I walked to the door. It wasn't doing any good to stay there.

"I love you, Elaine," I said quietly. "I'm not really in trouble. A long time ago I worked for a man. A big and important man. I guess you'd call him a gangster. I owe my life to him. Now I'm going to pay an installment on it. The last payment, I hope."

I opened the door. She tried to stop me. "No, Pete! Whatever it is, don't go!"

I kept walking, out to the car. She followed me, caught my arm. "Please, Pete. It's all right, I'm not angry with you, just don't go, stay with me, please!"

"I'll come back," I said.

She was crying now. "What are you going to do?"

"This man I worked for, his name is Macy Barr. Somebody's trying to kill him. I've got to find out who. It's the only chance we've got, Elaine. This time I'll make sure the past stays dead. Believe me."

I held her suddenly and kissed her, then got into the car quickly. She watched me silently, holding both arms across her stomach, hurting too much to speak. I saw her image in the mirror as I drove away, then the drive twisted and I couldn't see her any more. Once I thought I heard her call me, but maybe it was just a sound I made myself.

Rudy and I drove south fast. I discouraged conversation. I was thinking of how Macy had always had his way, even though it seemed for a while that I might make it stick when I went to him that day and told him I was quitting.

He had looked up at me irritably when I said it, as if I were trying to be funny in a way he didn't appreciate.

"You're what?"

I told him again. "I'm leaving," I said.

He looked at me with his eyes narrowing but spoke calmly. "Oh? Where do you think you're going?"

"I'm not sure. Upstate somewhere. Where I can lie in the sun and fish if I feel like."

He was playing along with me now, not sure how serious I was. "Then what?"

"Get a job. Work with my hands. A construction job, maybe. Something useful. I'd like that."

His mouth opened and closed. He couldn't cope with this right away. Nobody had ever tried to talk to him like that. I should have been scared but I wasn't. I was perfectly calm. Maybe that helped put it over. That and the fact that he knew me well and liked me.

"What's the matter? Don't I pay you enough?" He was

looking for a reason he could understand, and so was defeated already.

"You pay me enough."

He picked up a pencil and turned it over rapidly in his big fingers. His eyes were hard and chill, like ice on marble. "I'll be damned," he said, somewhat awed. "Five years, and then you turn up in here one morning and tell me you're through." His lips formed a stubborn, dangerous line. "You know more about me than any man alive. You don't just quit. What's the matter with you?"

"I quit," I said.

He looked at me steadily for over a minute, then I could see the doubt in his eyes, and the lines of his mouth soften. "You…kid," he said. "You…punk kid. College boy. Trouble with you is, you got too much education. Too many ideas crammed into your brain. Like your dad." He spread his hands. "Why? Just tell me why. Tell me something reasonable. You're not happy?"

"No. I'm not happy. I don't know if I ever will be. Maybe it's not important. Maybe I just want a change. My side of life has always been the side with its face in the gutter. I'm tired of neon sunsets and living at night. Maybe I want a woman who's never been rented out like a lending library book."

He lit a cigarette and watched the match burn, the charred wood curling slowly like a dying thing. "You nut. A regular nut. That's what I got. I kept you from drinking yourself to death once, didn't I, boy?"

I nodded. He seemed about to go on, then caught his breath. "Oh, what the hell. I can't say nothin' to you. You might as well go. Feeling the way you do you wouldn't be no good to me. I never understood you. You're the biggest screwball I ever knew. Sometimes I think you could tell me to spit and make me like it. You shouldn't have any trouble. They don't even have your phone number downtown you're so clean."

When I hesitated he told me to get out. He stopped me with a word when I reached the door.

"You know Lollipop, Pete?"

There was a hard surge of fear to smother the rising happiness and relief I was feeling. "I know what it stands for."

"I'm soft in the head for letting you walk out on me alive," he said tonelessly. "Maybe I got to know you too well. Maybe I'm soft because of your old man, remembering what a hell of a good lawyer he was—"

"Don't talk to me about the bastard."

"Don't ever give me reason to call somebody like Lollipop," he finished. "I can't help how much you know. But I can do something about it. Remember that!"

"I'll remember," I said.

I flipped a cigarette stub into the cool air streaming outside the car window, put my face into my hands, trying to press the ache from my eyes with my fingertips. For many months I had slept with a revolver tied to my wrist, always careful of the strangers around me, of the shadows at my back. No one ever came. Gradually I learned how to forget the way it had been: the tense crowded nights, living at the edge of a scream, nerves straining and alert for a look, a footstep, a gleam of light on knife or gun; trusting nothing, not the secretive men who gave information in whispers, nor the whisky drunk in locked bedrooms in a vain hope for relaxation, nor the silken flesh and long hot touch of many women.

"What's it like down there now?" I asked Rudy.

"There's a squeeze on," he said, glancing at me. "Stan Maxine's behind it. You remember Stan?"

"I remember him," I said dryly.

"Stan's a big boy now. Got a taste for big money. He has an idea that Macy runs too much. Maxine's got important friends upstairs. Guys who believe in taking care of their own. Macy's owned South Florida for years but he doesn't come from north of the Mediterranean and some of the wheels resent that. They wouldn't try to move one of their own boys into Macy's territory but if Maxine cut in they'd look the other way."

"Why doesn't Macy slap him down?"

Rudy shook his head slowly. "Who knows?" He paused, hunting for the right way to tell me what was on his mind. "You know how it was when you were with him, Pete. Macy owned everything then. He got his cut on every drop of bootleg, every deck of morph and stick of tea, every policy slip. There wasn't any two-bit gambler or waterfront loan shark who wasn't under Macy's thumb. He told everybody what to do. From the crummiest cat house to police headquarters to the union halls. Macy musta owned a thousand people in five or six counties."

"You trying to say Macy doesn't run the show any more?"

"Not like he used to. I just run errands nowadays, I'm not on the inside like you used to be. But I can tell Macy's slipping. He had a couple of props knocked out from under him. When you got as much territory as Macy does, you got to work hard and have some smart boys to keep the organization clicking. But he never found any-body as good as you to check on the boys up the line and finger the ones who were pocketing more than their share of the gravy, cheating Macy on the cut. Then there was a shakeup in coptown and some of Macy's pals got kicked out. Macy had to sweat out a local crime commission probe and close down gambling here and there until things cooled some. All those guys were interested in was gambling and a couple of murders and they didn't touch anything else. But it threw Macy off stride and it seems like he never caught up. Sometimes I think he don't care. He stopped working so hard. Took trips. Stayed down at his place on the island a lot instead of in town.

"Then word got around that he wasn't so tough any more and the boys started cheating him blind.

"Anyhow that's what I've heard. The cuts aren't so fat these days. Hard times, the boys say. But I hear the bootleg and dope shipments haven't slowed down none. Maxine's watched this going on and now he's starting to feel his muscle."

"And Macy's not doing anything about it?"

"Right now he and Maxine are sort of watching each other. Smiles with a gun in the pocket. See?"

"Cold war, huh?"

"Like that."

I sat back, thinking about Macy Barr. Things were going bad for him. Once he had been absolute, a ruthless tyrant in a tiny rich empire, who would roll up his sleeves and use his own hands on those it was necessary to impress with his power. Now he was beginning to feel his years. Maybe Maxine would get him. Maybe it would be the Treasury boys finding chinks in the legitimate front constructed over the years by a squad of expensive lawyers. At any rate, somebody would get him, because once his kind of luck began to sour he was finished.

I had a different life now. I didn't want to step back into his. I didn't want to die along with him. But it wasn't my choice to make. I felt helpless. Resentment heated my throat. Each passing mile shoved me deeper into the web from which I might not escape. After this job there would be others. Macy would find a reason to keep me around. I swallowed grimly. I'd kill him myself before I'd let that happen.

Rudy pushed the big Pontiac hard along the wide highway, hitting better than ninety, slowing as little as possible for the clusters of towns that were little more than winking traffic lights, darkened buildings, bright angles of neon. Outside of Port Wentworth the highway widened by two lanes illuminated by tall curved posts tipped with dazzling bluish lights. We were in an industrial suburb. Long blocks of warehouses with small windows stretched along the roadway behind chain-link fencing. Half a mile ahead red warning beacons winked atop huge silver globes in a chemical storage yard.

My eyelids were heavy and I thought about closing my eyes to rest them. Instead I reached for a cigarette. If I had closed my eyes, my face would have been shot off in another minute.

A hundred yards ahead a car spurted onto the highway and stopped directly in the path of the speeding Pontiac. In the second it took Rudy to whip out a curse and put his foot to the brake we had traveled a third of that distance. I glanced at the speedometer. We were going 105 miles an hour. Try to stop a car going that fast in two hundred feet. Rudy knew it, too, and I heard him groan helplessly as we skidded toward the other car. It was a black Ford,

I saw now. I saw something else, too, as Rudy wrestled with the wheel, trying to ease the Pontiac to the other side of the highway. The tires were screaming. I ducked below the dash an instant before the right side of the windshield was blasted out with a shotgun aimed from the Ford.

Rudy yelled and I felt the car lurch as it shot across the corrugated safety zone. I barely straightened up, and had no time to grab the wheel, as the heavy car plunged down an embankment. In the space of a heartbeat, the Pontiac hit, throwing me against the dash. I saw one of the concrete lamp posts rush toward us, then veer to one side. We hadn't slowed down much. There was a hideous shrieking sound of torn metal as the post was sideswiped. The car rocked, the back end starting to swing around as we slammed through a board fence. Something hit my head. The seat seemed to tip sharply and throw me out. I had no sensation of hitting the concrete pavement inside the fence.

Through a hot black fog I heard a vague roaring. I moved a hand and an arm and touched my face. Lights swished by my eyes, appearing and receding in the fog. I hurt everywhere. The thought of the Ford and the shotgun put me on my feet. There was blood on the back of my hand. I didn't know where it had come from. I shut my eyes tightly, opened them, steadied my swaying body.

Twenty-five yards behind me the Pontiac—what was left of it—was burning at the base of one of the storage tanks. I didn't have time to worry about that, or about Rudy. The Ford was parked on the highway at the edge of the embankment we had driven down and a man stood beside the open door, raising a rifle to his shoulder. I could see him well. He was wearing some kind of pale blue hat with a light-colored band.

I tried to run but fell and rolled away as a sharp cracking sound jumped the distance between us and a rifle bullet screamed off the concrete where he had corrected for me. He was good and quick. With the car burning behind me I was better than a target hung on a wall. I got up and took a couple of steps and he shot again. He was low. The slug hit the heel of my shoe and knocked me down. I knew he wouldn't miss again. Rudy was yelling, but I was too busy to listen.

I had my own gun but the short barrel made it useless from that distance. A boxcar parked a hundred feet away on a siding offered cover. I started to crawl desperately that way, looking back over my shoulder at him. My throat was dried up tight. The only thing that was in my mind was the pale blue hat and a vision of Elaine running along the beach.

From somewhere another rifle was fired, two shots, a second apart, and one window of the Ford splintered. The gunman looked at it, looked away from me in confusion, the rifle resting on his forearm, butt against his side. A third shot sent him sprawling inside his car. The automobile was in motion before he pulled the door shut and tires screeched as the driver threw the Ford into a tight turn in the middle of the highway. There was a distant sound of sirens.

I turned and saw Rudy crouched behind the burning car, holding a carbine. "Get out of there, Rudy!" I yelled at him.

He backed away from the Pontiac and one leg buckled. If the car was going to blow up, it would have done so

before, but the heat from the flames was apt to set off the
storage tank above it. I limped toward him, feeling the
heat against my face. He was sitting on the concrete with
the carbine between his knees, his face full of pain. I took
him under the arms and lifted him, sliding him away,
toward the boxcar.

"Thanks," Rudy said, coughing wildly. "Something with
the...leg. Be all right, I suppose."

Big red trucks were roaring through a gate nearby,
trailing slack hose. I picked up the rifle and my revolver
and threw them into the boxcar. I started back toward the
wrecked automobile. Rudy stopped me for a second. His
face was streaked with dirt and dripping perspiration and
blood. His eyes were frightened behind the dirty lenses
of his glasses.

"Now you see?" he choked. "Now you see why you had
to come back, Pete?"

Chapter Four

Macy Barr's home was on a small island thirty miles south of Castile. The island was about three hundred yards from shore, accessible by an old causeway barely wide enough for one car. At the island end of the causeway was a small house of weathered coquina, and an eight-foot gate consisting of heavy fence wire woven inside an iron frame. I hit the horn and turned off the headlights as Rudy instructed. A big spotlight on the building brightened the inside of the rented automobile.

A man carrying a submachine gun came out of the gatehouse and opened the gate. I drove through, followed a winding drive up an incline to the house and parked near a large garage. Rudy was nursing his head with an ice pack and didn't say anything.

We unloaded charred suitcases and went inside. It was a nice house, two floors and various levels, a cross between modern and Mediterranean, built to take advantage of every stray breeze. We left the luggage in the spacious foyer, and Rudy, after looking at his watch, showed me to Macy Barr's room. The effort of every step marked his face.

Macy wore an old faded bathrobe over a heavy frame that had gone to fat. He needed a haircut and a shave. He sat in an old armchair as shabby as he was and watched me with soft burning eyes. Then he looked at Rudy leaning against a wall behind me.

"What happened to you?" he said. Every breath he took made a faint husking noise in his throat.

"We were bushwhacked outside of Port Wentworth," I said. "Two or maybe three in on it. One to phone ahead. They used a shotgun and then they used a rifle. The Pontiac cracked up and fire gutted it. Rudy hauled a carbine from under the dash and ran them off. The Wentworth cops let us go when they checked the registration. They told us to keep our family fights down south so their citizens don't get hurt."

Macy cleared his throat thoughtfully. His eyes burned like dying coals. There were ugly smears of darkened skin under the eyes. "You hurt?" He meant both of us.

"I lost some skin when I went out of the car. Contusions everywhere. Rudy got burned some, pulled a muscle in his leg. We were lucky."

"Nerves shot to hell," Rudy said through his teeth.

"Who were they?" Macy sat stiffly in the chair, not moving a finger.

"I don't know. Neither does Rudy. I got a look at one of them, the lad with the rifle. A chunky bastard wearing a sky-blue hat. I'll know him again when I see him."

Macy moved then, looked at his thumbs. His lips folded together loosely, pinched down at the corners. His chest heaved a couple of times beneath the old robe. I wondered why he still wore the thing. They were putting better material in sugar sacks these days. I heard Rudy coughing delicately, as if every cough cost him pain.

"You go on to bed," Macy told Rudy. "Better get a hot bath." Rudy went out. "You want a drink, Pete?"

"God, yes."

He waved me to a small bar. I chose a bottle. "Give me some whisky," he said.

"What you want in it?" I said.

"I don't want nothing in it!" he said peevishly.

I gave him some whisky. He held it as somebody else might hold a rare flower. He drank it slowly. In between sips I could hear the breath in his throat.

I mixed one for myself. There wasn't any ice so I did without. I sat on his bed and looked at him sullenly.

"I'm glad you're back, Pete," he said. I didn't say a word. "Sorry you ran into trouble on the way down."

"Maybe you got some idea who planned it," I said.

"No. I ain't had any trouble like that." He tapped his long fingernails against the glass. It was good crystal that must have cost two hundred for the set. Tapping it produced a clear lingering sound. "So you're not happy," he said. "I can't help it."

"Let me tell you how happy I am," I said, getting up. "Six years ago I walked out on you because I was sick of you and your whole rotten business. I tried to forget you. I met a nice girl who didn't know what a fix was, who didn't know men were murdered every day in this country because guys like you can pull strings. I love her as I never loved anybody before. I used the money you paid me because I earned that money and I built a little business and bought a home against the day I'd be married, and tried to behave like a normal, everyday kind of guy. It was hard because at first I was acting. Then I began to feel that it was coming out all right, that the old life hadn't scarred me too deep."

I paused for breath. I didn't take my eyes off him. The

muscles of my jaw were tight. "I was beginning to feel happy. You know what that is, to be happy? To me it meant those little things like spending a lazy day on some shady canal with a fishing rod or chinning with the customers in my store for hours on end. These things gave me a satisfaction I had never known before. When things go right for you it's like nothing ever was wrong or ever can be. Then Rudy showed up and all the good things fell apart. I had to come back with him. You had it fixed so I'd have no choice. You knew any other way I would have told you to cram it. You knew a beating wouldn't have changed my mind. So you took the filthiest hook you could find to bring me back."

"Why don't you sit down?" he said wearily.

"I'm not quite through. I come back and what do I find? Not Macy. Not the old Macy. You used to be a pretty hard guy. You used to be as tough as any of the thugs you had working under you. There wasn't any one of them could make you back down. Now you're fat and out of shape and you sit in that chair feeling sorry for yourself when you should be back in town running things as if you meant it."

A little fire colored his cheeks. "You think I'm soft? I can take care of you any day, big shot. I give away a lot of years but I can handle you and anybody else!"

"Get out of that chair and prove it!"

He started to get up, then his expression became thoughtful and a little sheepish, and he slumped back. "Aw, what the hell we talkin' about?" he said. "We a couple of kids that we got to show how goddam tough we are? Sit down, you bastard. I knew you when you were in grammar school. Don't try to impress me. I said *sit down!*"

I sat on the edge of the bed, holding the glass tightly.

"You gonna do a job for me or are you gonna sit around and pout?"

"I'm going to do a job," I said, "because I can't do anything else."

"I don't care what your goddam reasons are!" he snapped. Then, more calmly, he said, "All right. We work on that basis. You don't like it but you do it because Macy says you do it. So naturally you don't like Macy. But I don't want nothin' half-ass."

"You'll get your dollar's worth," I said.

"I always did, with you," Macy said grudgingly. "Okay. Rudy tell you what I want? Put up that damn glass before you bust it."

I put up the glass. He was still giving orders with every breath, but they didn't have the old cocksure ring of authority.

"You been getting letters with the same message," I said. "Somebody's sore at you for burning out a tailor's shop twenty-five years ago and killing a few people. He's getting even by hunting down your old gang and knifing them. You're on the list but he's saving you until you've had time to think about it."

Macy nodded morosely. "There's an envelope in the middle drawer of that desk over there. Get it, will you, Pete?"

The envelope contained all the clippings Macy had received. I read one of them about the fire. The tailor's name was Kennedy. He had a wife and two children. Nobody knew how the fire started. One of the children somehow survived, was in the hospital with serious burns. The child's name wasn't given.

Macy told me to keep the envelope. "What happened to the other kid?" I asked him.

He seemed indifferent. "I don't know. I haven't looked into this thing. That's your job."

"You worry about anything at all these days?" I said bitingly. He looked at me with a flash of anger in his eyes but didn't speak.

"What chance that Stan Maxine's behind this?" I said.

"No chance. He wouldn't be so cute. Stan don't know how to be subtle-like. It ain't his way of doing things."

"I hear he's got fat and happy lately. You should have killed him a dozen years ago. I should have killed him. I never killed anybody in my life, not counting the war, but if I had to choose somebody it would be Maxine."

Macy smiled slightly. "You ain't changed so much," he said in a low thick voice. "You're older, but your face don't show it. You got a girl now."

I nodded.

He looked up at me eagerly. "A real beauty? I know she must be. I'll bet she's a smart one, too, and knows how to talk, and things like that. She knows about you?"

"No, I never told her." I cut it short. "What about Maxine?"

"Maxine?"

"Why don't you stand up to him now, before he gets too hard to handle. Boot his tail back where it belongs."

"I'm afraid to try," he said, watching me almost ashamedly. "I'm afraid to find out I'm not strong enough any more. Sometimes it's better just to hang on, Pete."

He got up then and went to the window. One of his pockets was bulky with a gun. He pulled the blinds open and looked out at the moon shining on the dark sea.

"I'll be working alone," I said. "I'll need a car." He nodded. "How many men have you got around?"

"Three. Rudy and two other boys, Reavis and Taggart. Top guns. Taggart's not around right now. I sent him to Tampa yesterday. He should pull in before long."

"Not enough to carry your coffin."

His shoulders flexed. "Nobody's going to kill me, Pete. Not while I'm here. Your room's in the west wing, just off the patio, if you want to go on to bed." He spoke tiredly, dismissing me. I picked up the envelope with the newspaper clippings and went downstairs.

Chapter Five

I unpacked most of the clothes from the suitcase, then threw it and the ruined stuff away. My other suit wasn't bad and I decided I could still wear it.

I turned down the covers on the bed but felt no need for sleep. It was going on a quarter of three. I washed my face carefully in warm water, left the room. There were French doors at the end of the hall and, beyond, a small patio and terrace surrounded by a low rock wall. I went out there. It was a hot night, the air not moving at all. My clothes smelled of smoke and sweat. I walked down the long sloping terrace to the bay beach, stood there and listened to the rippling of water against the sand.

Then I took off trousers and shirt, looked back toward the house. There was no moon at the moment, few lights in the windows. I took off my shoes and socks and the sand was smooth against my feet. Then I removed my damp underwear and stood naked at the edge of the water for a few moments before wading thigh-deep and swimming slowly. Muscles relaxed as I eased over on my back and floated. The scraped places on my arms stung and throbbed. Once I heard a plopping splash nearby, and thought of fish.

When I had cooled enough I swam back to the beach and waded in. I sat in the sand for a while, drying slowly in the humid air. The first time I heard the sound behind

me I ignored it. When I heard it again—the sound of
someone walking stealthily toward me in the sand—I
rolled on my belly, gathered my legs beneath me and
dived at an indistinct figure five feet away. We went
down. There was a muffled sound of surprise that I didn't
make. My hand slid along a smooth curved thigh, touched
rounded breasts and full nipples. I was holding a woman
as naked as I was, and holding her damned tight, the
weight of my body pinning her to the sand. She was rigid,
apparently too shocked to struggle. I backed away from
her fast and she sat up. I couldn't see her well, but I knew
she was beautifully proportioned, and I had an idea that
her hair was blonde. She cried out again, reached toward
her breasts with protective hands.

"I'm sorry," I said. "You shouldn't have come up behind
me like that."

For a few seconds she didn't speak. She sat in the
sand, legs crossed at the ankles. "It's...all right," she said
in a strained voice. "I'm sorry I...startled you." Her
hands came away from her breasts slowly and dropped to
her knees. She sat very still, apparently looking toward
me. I hadn't held her long, but long enough for her to be
perfectly aware I wasn't dressed either. Not that it made
any difference, in the dark.

"Who are you?" I said.

"I'm Diane. You...must be Pete. Pete Mallory."

"That's right."

"I've been swimming, too. I was in the water when you
came down here." She paused. "I don't sleep well."

I swallowed something hanging in my throat. I could
see just enough of her to make me wish I could see more.
The face was probably beautiful. The bone structure

seemed good. She made no effort to move further away from me.

"How did you know me?"

She turned her head so that I could see the curve of her throat. "I know everyone else who is here. I didn't recognize you. Macy's talked about you. He brought you here to find the person who's going to kill him."

"Yes."

She was silent for a moment. Then, "Do you have a cigarette, Pete?"

I went to my clothes and took a pack from the shirt, and matches. I returned to her, lit one, held it to her, seeing her features emerge in a scarlet glow. A fierce look narrowed her eyes as a hand hit the inside of my wrist hard, knuckles sharp against the tendons. The cigarette spun to the sand, glowed bravely for an instant, went out.

"You don't need to look," she said crossly.

I was surprised. She got to her feet stiffly. "I've seen it all before," I told her.

She stood for a long time without paying any attention to me, not even looking in my direction. I had been right in my guess. She was beautiful. The skin of her face was smooth and unlined, lips full and shaped for hungry kisses. Then she stretched, rising to her toes, and relaxed. Her voice was calm again.

"Macy will tell you about me," she said. "I'm supposed to be a little bit crazy."

"Are you?"

She laughed girlishly. "I suppose so. I suppose I am. But I'm harmless. Macy must think I'm all right. He trusts me to take care of Aimee."

"Aimee? Who's that?"

"You'll meet her in the morning. You'll like her. She's a lot like me. She has a wildness like me, tied down inside." She turned toward the bay. "Right now I want to go swimming."

"You ought to wear more clothes around here," I advised.

She laughed again. "It doesn't make any difference. Nobody will touch me. Macy wouldn't let them. Besides, I told you I'm supposed to be a little bit crazy."

She walked close to me, and I felt her fingers light against my shoulders. I had the scent of her and my heart beat too fast.

"I like you, Pete," she whispered to me, and then she was gone, running through the sand to the water and diving in with a hushed splash.

I pulled on my pants and slipped into socks and shoes, walked leisurely back to the house with my shirt over my arm.

Chapter Six

On the terrace I looked down the drive. Through the trees I saw a thin border of light in one window of the small gabled gatehouse. The thought of sleep wasn't right for me yet and the thought of Elaine was a gathering misery deep in my stomach, so I walked down the drive and knocked at the door.

"Who is it?" Rudy said. I told him. He came and opened the door timidly. He wore nothing but the old hat and a pair of underwear shorts pulled high over his sagging, stuck-out belly. In one hand he held an Italian automatic. His pinkish skin glistened wetly.

It was hot in the one-room house. The windows were open but Rudy had drawn the blinds. A slow-turning fan kept the air from becoming stifling. On a hot plate coffee bubbled in a glass percolator.

He offered me a chair and sat down in another, stuck the automatic into a shoulder holster hanging by the strap from the back of the chair.

"Where's the other fellow?" I asked Rudy.

"Reavis? Up at the house. One of us always sleeps in the room next to Macy's."

"Feel any better?"

He shook his head. "I cleaned up. I won't be able to move tomorrow."

"Thought you'd be in bed by this time."

He gave me a bleary look. "I don't sleep much these days."

"That gate outside doesn't look very sturdy to me. Fence wire won't hold back anybody who wants in bad enough."

He chuckled and got to his feet. "Want to see something?" There was a small control panel with three knife switches beside the door. Rudy pried one up. He opened the door. Outside, tiny spurts of blue flame along the wires accompanied the crisp sounds of frying insects. Rudy shut the heavy door and locked it, turned off the electricity.

"Enough juice to kill a cow," he said. "There's a fence operating on another circuit slung halfway around this island."

"Why no sleep, Rudy? You waiting for somebody to come along?" I was sorry for the cruelty in my voice.

"Get off it, will you?" he said. His tone was defeated. "You saw what happened tonight. I almost got it tonight. You would have got it right along with me if I hadn't been able to drag that carbine from under the dash." He took the percolator from the hot plate and poured coffee. He had to hold the cup close to his face to keep from spilling too much as he drank. As it was, some of the coffee trickled through the discolored hairs of his chest and stomach. He didn't bother to wipe the drops away.

"You been around a long time, Rudy," I told him. "You won't be as easy to get to as the others were."

He banged the cup against the table. "This guy," he said, swallowing hard, "this guy—" His eyes wandered helplessly as he tried to find the right words to tell me what he was feeling, what had been building inside him as he saw himself earmarked for a quick, bloody death. "I

been around *too* long, Pete," he said. "I've slowed down.
I've known too many other guys, quicker and smarter
than me, who couldn't find any place to hide once the
finger was on them. Oh, he'll get me, all right. He'll get
me." His fingers touched the butt of the automatic, lifted
convulsively. "Unless you—"

"How many people in the house knew which road
you'd take tonight?" I asked him.

His shoulders lifted. "It was no secret around here
that I was going to Orange Bay."

"Who's living here besides Macy?" I thought of Diane,
the girl I hadn't been able to see quite well enough. "He
got a woman around?"

"Macy? No. He don't care nothin' about women any
more. Once in a while I guess he can use one. Like me. I
got to rub up against one all night before I—"

"There's a girl I met on the beach a few minutes ago.
She was swimming."

"Diane."

"That's her name."

"She takes care of the kid. Aimee."

"Who is this Aimee?"

Rudy scratched fingers through his hair. "Macy's pet.
A little nine-year-old girl. She's Cuban, I think."

"How'd he come by that?"

"You remember Chilly Rosales?"

"Yeah."

"One of Chilly's cousins was a Spanish Town whore.
This Aimee was her kid. The whore's husband may or
may not have been her father. He wasn't home much.
One night when he was home he took a butcher knife and
cut up the whore. Aimee was watching. Then he went

after the kid and chased her down three flights of stairs. He got close enough once to take a swipe at her and opened one of her arms from the elbow down. So there they were, both of them bloody as Jesus and the girl screaming and running out into the street. A cop heard the screaming and shot the guy dead. Since the whore was his cousin, Chilly took care of the girl for a while, until he creamed himself and his Cadillac in an accident one night."

"Then Macy took her in," I said, grinning crookedly.

"Well," Rudy replied, "he said she needed to have somebody. She was wild as hell when he latched onto her. Diane toned her down. Took a long time."

"I'll be damned," I said, shaking my head in astonishment.

"Yeah."

"Who else is around, then?"

"Well, Diane and Aimee. Macy's brother Owen, too. He's supposed to be manager of the hotel but he don't do nothin' but booze and paint those pictures of his. Charley Rinke's here, too, with his wife."

It was a new name. "He's sort of like you used to be," Rudy explained, "except he ain't big enough or mean enough to handle the contact work. Rides the books, mostly. There's something about him I don't like much. He struts, you know, like he was real dangerous, especially around people who don't know no better, but any trouble and he's the first to find some place where it's safe to watch. I don't think even his wife likes him. She's been laid by some of the boys in town, especially Reavis. He does most of the heavy work these days, like collecting."

I felt the first quieting nudge of sleep, and stirred sore

muscles in getting up. "I think I'll turn in. See you in the morning, Rudy."

He went to the door with me. "How did you ever happen to go to work for Macy, Pete?" he asked suddenly.

I considered that for a while. "I guess Aimee wasn't the first lost kid Macy ever took in," I said, and walked outside.

Going up the hill, I thought about the way it had been; coming home from the war with each nerve bare from the endless nights of patrol and attack and retreat to find Jean, the wild beauty I had married at the end of college, slowly becoming a hopeless paretic. And nothing, nothing could stop the pitting of the brain that gradually turned her into a strange creature, with a halting walk and thick speech and weird hallucinations. I lasted long enough to see that she would be taken care of in the best institution I could afford. Then I cracked up. There were no memories for a while, not until Macy found me in some rathole, half-dead from whisky and grief, and flew me south to a small island in the Caribbean where I had the chance to start living again if I wanted to take it.

I remembered the day I stood high on a cliff, a storm blowing toward me from off the choppy sea, the wind high. Macy was yelling in my ear, his coat and tie whipping, hair in his face. He had a bottle in his hand and as he argued with me he raised his arm and threw the bottle over the cliff.

"You want another drink? If that's what you want, go get it! I'm tired of fooling around with you. You got any guts, go get that bottle!"

And I stood there, shaking, cold, squeezing my face with my hands, wondering why it was so hard for me to take those steps that would end it. I stood there a long time until I wasn't trembling any more. Then I turned and walked away from the edge of the cliff. I didn't feel good because I was doing it. I didn't feel as though I had won any great victory over myself. I didn't feel anything.

"Where do you think you're going?" Macy had said with a grin.

I turned and looked back at him. "With you, if you want me. If not, I don't know where."

But too many wires had pulled loose for me to hope that I could live normally again before many years. I needed the feeling of danger that the job with Macy offered me—until the healing was complete. Then I left him.

Chapter Seven

A woman was asleep on my bed when I opened the door of the room. Apparently she had been sleeping fitfully because she sat up, squinting painfully, as soon as I turned on the light. She seemed to be about thirty years old, small and tightly knit, with hair like dull gold. Without the puffiness under the eyes and the tension lines on her face, she would have been beautiful.

"Please turn it out," she said, almost moaning. "It hurts my eyes."

I turned off the overhead, switched on a small pin-up lamp over the dresser, throwing long searching shadows through the room.

"I didn't know anyone was using this room," she said, blinking. She sat tensely on the edge of the bed, as if constantly aware of some internal tightening. She wore a filmy pale green nightgown that dropped like a curtain from the mounds of her breasts to her lap. Her nipples showed prominently through the material. Glancing down, she became aware of her body and, without any fuss, took a robe from the floor and put it about her shoulders, drawing it shut indifferently, as if it didn't matter whether I looked or not.

"I couldn't sleep in my room," she said. "I walked around the house and came in here and just lay down." She looked at me. "I'm Evelyn Rinke," she said.

I put my shirt over the back of a chair. "Pete Mallory."

Her eyes inspected me openly and with great care. She seemed to have no embarrassment. The set of her mouth and sleepy eyes reminded me of a hungry young bird. "Yes," she said. "I knew you were coming. I've heard them talk about you."

She got up slowly, walked toward me and around me. "I guess you want to go to bed. You must be tired." She tilted her head slightly, looked up at me. Her lips parted and I saw her tongue against her teeth. She stepped closer to me, her fingers grasping my arms, sliding over the elbows, along the flat muscles. Her fingers were long and hard, hot and dry. They tightened, relaxed. She drew her body against me, the material of the nightgown rasping softly. There was no softness about her body, no fleshiness. It was as hard as the fingers, had a feeling of strength, as if it could be used again and again with no slackening of the lean tight muscles. I could feel her trembling, feel her warm, vaguely sweet breath come in gusts. It wasn't passion that made her tremble. Her eyes were restless and wild. She wanted me to put my hands on that body and gentle it, and then do with it as I pleased.

"Let me go to bed with you," she said. "Let me sleep with you. I really need to. I need to sleep next to a man for a change."

I took her arms and moved her away from me. She was beginning to perspire lightly. Tiny drops appeared on her forehead. Her fingers squeezed once again, then she backed away still more. Her eyes were cloudy. She didn't seem upset that I had refused her, just disappointed. In withdrawing her fingertips, she touched the scraped places along my forearms. I looked at them. They were stippled with dried blood. Most of it had washed off during my swim.

"You're hurt," she said. "How did that happen?"

"I was trying to run away. Somebody was shooting at me."

Her expressive eyebrows pressed down. "Does that happen often?"

"No. It hasn't lately. Not since the war." She wasn't standing still now, but moving as though something inside was whipping at her. She breathed deeply.

"What's your trouble?" I asked. "Nerves?"

"God, yes." Her fingers clenched. "God, yes."

"I know," I said. "I had the same trouble once. The war did it to me."

Mrs. Rinke smiled painfully. "Wars always end. I wish something that simple could help me. I'd drink, if it didn't make me sick. How I'd drink!"

She looked at the pavement burns on my arms again. "I'll get something for those," she said, and left before I could protest. She was back before long with a white metal first-aid kit. She used an antiseptic on the scrapes, doctored them with iodine.

"Better not bandage them," she said. "They'll heal faster."

I looked up to see a man standing in the doorway. He wore loose pajamas and no robe. Evelyn Rinke was too engrossed in repacking the first-aid kit to notice him. He was a little man, slightly built, with pale hair in a crew cut and thick glasses that made his grayish-purple eyes round and staring. His ears were big and his jaws long and hollowed beneath strong wide cheekbones. The mouth was too large for his face, and folded down at the edges when it ran out of room. The upper lip was thin and almost bloodless, slanted down from the cleft, corners fitting into deep pockets. His lips had a certain acid primness, like those of an obnoxious preacher. But his voice was firm and soft and polite, betraying no irritation from finding his wife in my room.

"I missed you, Evelyn," he said. He was looking at me. "You weren't in your bed."

She was startled. She jerked around, pulling the robe together. Her fingers clamped tightly together at her belly. The small pleasure she had taken from helping me cleanse my scraped arms fled.

"I...couldn't sleep, Charley. It was warm, and...I couldn't sleep. Mr. Mallory was hurt. I..."

Rinke walked toward me and offered his hand. He apparently wasn't bothered by the fact that his wife's body had been prominently visible through the nightgown under the carelessly worn robe.

He shook hands with me strongly. "I've heard a lot about you," he said. "From Macy." His mouth told the tone of his thoughts. It stayed surly. "Macy thinks a lot of you," he went on. "I'm Charley Rinke. I suppose Macy told you about me."

"No, he didn't," I said. "I'm glad to meet you, Mr. Rinke."

"Oh?" It seemed to disturb him that Macy hadn't mentioned him. "I guess you'll be with us for a while, Mr. Mallory."

"Probably."

"I know you want to be left alone." He glanced at his wife. "You're not feeling well, Evelyn?"

She shook her head. Her agitation had become worse

since the sudden appearance of her husband.

"Did you have an accident, Mr. Mallory?" Rinke said, still looking at Evelyn. It was a trick he had, to look at one person and talk to another. He seemed interested.

"Sort of. I'm all right."

He waited for more information. When I didn't offer any he said, "Evelyn, a hot bath would help, wouldn't it?"

"I...I don't think so, Char—"

"But it has helped before, hasn't it?" he said, taking her by the arm. "It does relax you. Wouldn't you like to have a hot bath? I'll wash your back for you."

"Ch-Charley..." she said unhappily, her head hanging. She allowed herself to be guided toward the door.

"We'll be seeing you in the morning, Mr. Mallory," Rinke said pleasantly. Evelyn turned to me for a moment, and there was a glitter of anguish in her eyes, of a plea that had been ignored often. She tugged with her arm and he let her go quickly, followed her into the hall.

After a moment I shut the door and finished undressing, set the alarm for eight. It was ten after four then, but I wasn't there to catch up on my sleep.

Chapter Eight

I slept right through the alarm but a Puerto Rican house-boy shook me awake a few minutes later and got me out of the sack. He had to assist me in getting to the bathroom, then held me up under the shower until the feel of the water penetrated gritty layers of pain. I might have stayed under all day but he reminded me politely that Macy expected everyone to be at breakfast by eight-thirty. I shook my head gently to test the reliability of stiff muscles, and got out.

My fingers had trouble holding the razor and my wrist was rubber as I shaved. I felt like death warmed over. Clean clothes and hot coffee thoughtfully provided by the houseboy helped some. I made the dining room at twenty of nine. The others were eating. Macy looked up from a plateful of eggs and threw introductions around carelessly. Then he went back to eating.

I knew most of them. Only Rudy and Mrs. Rinke were absent. I took a vacant seat beside Rinke, looked at Diane more carefully. She was a tall lemon-haired blonde with a serene face every bit as beautiful as my quick look in the cigarette glow last night had suggested. She paid no attention to me. She was wearing shorts and some kind of pullover playshirt with elbow length split sleeves laced together and tied with little cord bows.

Next to her was Aimee, a thin, undersized little Cuban girl with straight black hair and a flat nose. Aimee and

Macy did most of the talking, back and forth across the table. Macy was in good spirits. He took great delight in learning everything the child had done the day before.

Aimee would twist her head from side to side and smile big but vaguely and answer in a few halting words. Her attention was easily distracted. Diane had to coax her patiently to eat.

"We gonna go boat riding 'safternoon, Daddy?" Aimee asked Macy, lifting a napkin to wipe away milk from the corner of her mouth. I noticed a wide glossy scar on her arm.

"Well, I don't know, dear," Macy said, with a slight frown. He looked better this morning, in a bright yellow sport shirt, his hair carefully combed and face shaved. He looked more like the old confident, angle-wise Macy. "You know I don't care for boats…"

Aimee stuck with it. "I haven't been boat riding all week." There was a trace of her ancestry in her speech.

"Diane can take you," Macy said, cutting up a piece of steak.

"But I want to go with you," Aimee said pathetically.

Macy reached across the table and patted her hand. "I know, baby. Well—" He scratched his jaw. "Maybe tomorrow. Daddy has to work today."

One of the servants brought me orange juice and a platter of steak and eggs. Rinke had said nothing to me when I sat down, only nodded, but when he was through eating he turned and asked, "How are you this morning, Mr. Mallory?"

"I'm hanging on." I remarked on the absence of his wife.

"Evelyn's not feeling well this morning. Her back is

giving her some pain." He turned his glum face away abruptly, put a cup of coffee to it. "Evelyn has a problem with her nerves," he said, sipping slowly. "She suffers a great deal. We've been unable to find anything that might help her." He put the cup down and straightened his glasses precisely. "I wanted to be sure you understood about Evelyn. About how she is."

"I think I know what you mean," I said.

He nodded, his large eyes on me. He blinked once, slowly.

"I'm engaged to be married, myself," I said.

He nodded again, and smiled disarmingly. "Is that so?" The news seemed to please him. "Is that right?" he said again, as if he were afraid I was only funning.

"I sure hope Mrs. Rinke feels better," I said.

"I'm sure she will." He got up then, having tugged at my heartstrings enough, and excused himself.

"You going into town, Pete?" Macy said through a mouthful.

"Yes."

Diane looked up and glanced at me fleetingly. "Could Aimee and I go in with Mallory?" she said to Macy.

"I'm going in later. I can take you," a new voice grumbled. It came from Taggart, Macy's hired hand, a formidable giant as solidly and thickly built as bridge piling. He was good-looking but his features had no mobility and his expression was gluey, turtle-slow.

"I wanted to go in earlier so I could take Aimee shopping after we leave the doctor," Diane explained. She touched the back of Taggart's brown hand. "You can pick us up at the department store this afternoon."

His face inclined toward his plate by half an inch. He

didn't look at the blonde girl. Her fingers touched his hand for a moment longer, then withdrew. Despite the lack of words, there seemed to be some bond of intimacy between them. He picked up a piece of bread and wiped up the egg yolk on his plate with it, crammed the bread into his mouth.

Most of them were through eating before I started. I had the dining room to myself when Owen Barr came in. I had forgotten that he was in the house. He wore a shiny purple bathrobe and flopping slippers. He was a little chunky man with red hair that stuck out here and there in tufts around his ears. The top of his head was bald. He had a bristly mustache and mean eyes. He looked worse than I felt.

He tottered to the table, grabbed the coffeepot and poured a slug into somebody else's cup. He drank it, sobbing a little between gulps. He looked at me while he was drinking, but not as if he saw me.

"God damn it," he said passionately. "Oh, God damn it." He walked around in a big circle, his slippers flopping, his short arms stuck out to balance him. Then he had another cup of coffee, after which he half sat in a chair and half leaned on his elbows against the table and held the cup tightly with stubby fingers and worked up a belch, a look of great concentration on his blotched face. Big drops of sweat appeared on his forehead.

I drank the last of my orange juice, left the room and went in search of Macy. I found him in a study in an air-conditioned wing of the house, his feet on the desk, reading the morning paper. There was a loaded .45 on the desk within easy reach. When he heard my step in the doorway he put the paper across the desk, covering the automatic and the hand that grasped it.

Then he looked at me, picked up the paper again, flicking ashes off a cigarette in his mouth with a corner of it.

"Ready to go?" he muttered.

"Yeah. I'll need a car. Rudy can return that rented job when he's up and around. Expense money, too."

"We got a lot of cars in the garage. Pick out one you like. Keys are in the ignition." He went to his wallet and counted out money for me.

"From now on you don't talk about what I'm doing," I said. "You don't tell anybody where I go or who I see. Is the phone bugged?"

He folded the paper and put it in his lap. "As far as I know, it isn't. Telephone company watches it to see the line stays clean. I trust everybody here, Pete."

I reached over and picked up the .45. "And you're using this for a paperweight." He didn't say anything. I took it by the barrel and threw it at him. He sat there holding it foolishly.

"I don't trust anybody," I said. "Nice little family you got here, Macy. The blonde in particular. Where did you get her?"

"Diane? Oh, I found her wandering around the hotel one night three or four years ago. Nearer four. She was looking for a job. Well, you know, I liked the way she was built. I thought I'd try to get me some, but when I went to peel her clothes off she threw a hysterical fit and said she'd kill me."

His eyes were fond with the memory of her and the

pleasures of younger times. "I didn't give up easy. I kept
her around, but I never could—you know, hardly even
touch her, she was so damn jumpy. Finally I got tired of
chasing her and passed her on to Maxine and told him to
put her to work somewhere. That was when I could still
tell him things. Later on when I had Aimee on my hands
I took her back because she was the only one who could
handle the kid."

"She a nut of some kind?"

"Oh, I don't know. Diane's probably a little off balance,
but harmless. She has these fits sometimes if people try
to push her. Or maybe she'll just sit around and stare and
not say a word. But she's really okay and she's good for
Aimee." He grinned. "How do you like Aimee? How do
you like that little monkey, huh?"

I was expected to like Aimee. "Cute. She has a look
like somebody chases her through her dreams."

He wagged his head. "Couple more years, she'll forget all about it. I've given her something here. Security.
She wakes up screaming now and she's not alone. She's
sleeping in a big bed with Diane, not on some piss-caked
cot in a stinkin' room. She's in a solid house with the
ocean outside singing her to sleep. I've done something
for her. She'll forget."

"What's she done to you?"

"Huh?" He looked at me stupidly, shaking loose the
clinging paternal thoughts.

"Skip it," I told him, and started toward the door.

"You let me know when you got something," he said,
far too casually. I could hear the tension in his voice.

"I'll let you know."

In my room I picked up a coat and put it on over my

sport shirt. I walked down the hall and ran into Owen Barr. He stopped and chugged back like a myopic beetle. He showed some signs of being conscious, so I spoke to him.

"Hello, Owen. You still managing the Coral Gardens for Macy?"

He looked up at me and almost snarled, "Get out of my way so I can go to my room, unless you'd rather I puke here in the hall." I sidestepped and he went rapidly along, tipping against the wall a couple of times. I shrugged and went outside to the garage.

Chapter Nine

Diane and Aimee were waiting for me at the garage. Diane had changed from shorts to a tweedy-looking green skirt and Aimee was wearing a pink and white dress and white shoes and looking as if she might be suffering from it.

I selected a Buick from the garage and they climbed in. Diane took sunglasses with heavy pink shell frames from her purse and put them on. Aimee regarded me steadily and inquisitively when she thought I wasn't likely to glance at her. She was wearing a bit of lipstick, Diane's shade. When we drove by the house Macy waved from the front porch and Aimee waved back, breaking out a smile for an instant. Then she sat forward on the edge of the seat with her small fingers curled over the dashboard and looked intently through the windshield.

Reavis let us through the high gate, having left his submachine gun inside the house out of respect to the ladies. This was my first look at him by daylight, and there wasn't much to see. Medium height and heavy in the chest, but in time the flesh would sag. He was a younger Rudy Mask.

"It's a beautiful morning," Diane said. "I hope we don't have to waste all of it in the doctor's office."

"What's Aimee going for?"

"Shots." Aimee almost flinched, her face troubled. Diane put an arm around her. "There's nothing to it, baby. Diane's going to get a couple herself."

"Then can we go to the show?" Aimee said insistently, as if she had been asking since waking up that morning.

"Maybe we'll have time. We have to eat lunch and see about your playsuits, too."

"And a bicycle."

Diane sighed. "I don't know where you're going to ride a bicycle around—"

"But Daddy said—"

"I know he did. I was just trying to be practical. We'll see about the bicycle, too."

"I want to see a Bob Hope picture."

"Sounds good to me," Diane said cheerfully. She smiled at me. "See how busy we'll be today. You should come with us."

"I can't take those shots. Pass out every time."

Aimee lapsed into stricken silence and Diane scowled at me, her eyes rolling in Aimee's direction. She fussed with the child's hair. Aimee began singing something to herself.

"Are you working today?" Diane said.

I nodded.

"What will you try first? I just don't see how you could track down someone like this. I've heard Macy talk about the newspaper clippings. They've been mailed from everywhere."

"I have to give it a try. There's always a place to start."

"Where will you start?"

I just smiled.

Diane pouted. "Trusting, aren't you?"

"No."

"What clippings, Diane?"

"Hush." She turned her face and I could see it out of

the corner of my eye—a very rare thing, fine bones and full, curved cheeks and clear creamy skin. No bumps, no marks. Small white teeth. "Well," she said, "if I was going to be the detective I know where I'd go first."

"Oh, you do?" Her good spirits were beginning to warm me.

She smiled smugly. "Yes. First of all I'd want to know about the child who didn't die. Then I'd want to find… relatives, friends. Persons like that. Maybe one of them has carried a grudge all these years."

"It's possible."

She hit me sharply on the leg. "You're hopeless."

"How has Macy felt about these newspaper stories?"

"Diane, *what* stories?"

"Now, we're talking about something—grown-up. Very stuffy."

Aimee bounced once on the rich leather seat cover and was still. We passed a parrot jungle and her eyes were large as she turned her head, catching glimpses of the bright-feathered birds. I slowed down so she could look.

"Can we go there sometime?" She bounced on the seat again.

"Sometime," Diane said. To me she said, "He's sort of acted like it was a joke. You know, the kind of joke somebody thinks is funny to make again and again but really isn't, only you laugh so people won't know you're irritated by it. He doesn't think anything can happen to him."

She looked away, not liking the questioning to be reversed. Her fingers reached out to the radio and she turned it on.

"Do you think you'll find this killer, Pete?" she asked, then, when Aimee looked curiously at her, apparently wished she hadn't said killer.

"I don't know." I slowed down, looked down the road, sped past a wobbly truck smoking like a clogged fireplace. "Maybe."

"You must be pretty good," Diane said. "I've heard Macy talk about you. He doesn't understand you, but he likes you. Maybe for the same reason I like you. Because you're not so easy to understand. You've a hard shiny surface around something that might be very good to know."

A guitar whanged furiously from the radio. An astonishing voice cried: *"...Down at the end of Lonely Street, that's—Heartbreak Hotel."* Diane made a face and changed stations.

"Easy, lady," I said, half-kidding, half-warning. I remembered the beach scene the night before, the long lush body, the touch of her fingertips.

She dug in her purse for cigarettes, found one and lit it. She offered a drag to me and I took it, passed the cigarette back.

"You married, Pete?"

"No. Engaged."

She smoked for a while, silently. Breeze from the rolled-down windows lifted her hair away from her neck. She smoothed it absently. "Why did you leave her to come back?"

"That's kind of a stupid question, coming from you. It wasn't because I wanted to."

"Let up on me, mister. The tone hurts."

"Sorry. I'm hurting, too." I wished she hadn't spoken.

Thinking about Elaine wasn't so good. It took my thoughts away from the job I had to do, so Macy could go on living. I wondered how Elaine would explain to her parents why I wasn't around, why I had to leave so suddenly for Castile. For a moment I regretted I hadn't told her everything. But it would only have caused her to worry more. My fingers ached from the tightness of my grip on the wheel. I knew now how others had felt when Macy's kind of pressure was applied. Like the city official who committed suicide. I could hate Macy now, where once there was only dislike.

"What has he got on you, Pete?" Diane asked.

"You know everything else," I said. "You should know that."

"That's not fair," she murmured, and turned from me to look out the window.

I wondered about her. By her own admission she wasn't normal. But nothing she had said or done in the brief time I had known her indicated any irrationality. She seemed shrewd and well-bred, with a spark of fun in her. From a purely physical standpoint, she was breathtaking. She could have been twenty-five or thirty. She was something of a mystery herself, and there were questions I wanted to ask her, and would, at a better time. I wanted to know why she was with Macy, why she had let herself be handed around like a piece of furniture.

Diane was very quiet now, and her face had a way of becoming smooth and still, without a flicker of animation, until it was like something painted with the greatest delicacy and closest attention to detail, but painted still. I knew that when the time would be right for the questions

I would find her protective coating as hard to crack as she claimed mine to be. I wondered what it would be like to make love to her, to hold the remarkable body captive, feel all its strength and softness and fire. I squelched the thought harshly. I recalled what Macy had said about her that morning. He had done nothing with her. But maybe she was a woman who chose her men as carefully as she chose fine clothes.

Yet Stan Maxine had had her for a while. When I had known him he was a young, ruthless hood with a dark unsavory look that many women had been dumbly, helplessly attracted to. I wondered how Diane had treated Stan, a greedy and avaricious lover.

"You worked for Stan Maxine a while, didn't you?" I asked her.

I thought for a moment she would ignore me. Then she said, "Yes. I was a cashier in his restaurant for a few months. Stan's restaurant is one of the favorites in Castile. Then I worked in the supply house for a while. Stan owns a firm that supplies linen to hotels and restaurants and bars."

It sounded like a nice front, and undoubtedly was a financially sound enterprise. I wondered how much rough work was necessary before hotel owners saw the advantages of Stan's service.

"Did you ever know Stan?"

"I knew him. A long time ago."

"I'll bet you didn't get along," she said.

"How did you get along with him?"

She finished the cigarette and tucked it into the dashboard ashtray. "I liked him," she said simply. "I still like him."

Castile's southernmost suburbs began to cluster beside the wide highway and traffic slowed. At Balmar I cut across town to the Mulloy Freeway and went into the city by way of the airport. Diane gave me the address of a clinic on Shrader Boulevard. I left her and Aimee there, and drove downtown to the *Sun-Express* building.

Chapter Ten

In the file room of the *Sun-Express* I found follow-up stories on the fire. One of them told me the lone survivor was a six-year-old named Carla Kennedy. She was the oldest of the three children. No mention was made of how she escaped the fire. The little girl had been badly burned and was recovering in Good Shepherd Hospital. None of the stories mentioned any relatives of the Kennedys.

The four clippings about the fire that Macy had received had been taken from the noon edition of the Castile *Sun*, dated May 19, 1932. The issues of the newspaper were preserved on microfilm.

At Good Shepherd Hospital I spent three quarters of an hour looking through boxes of old ledgers and records before I found out that Carla Kennedy had been discharged from the hospital thirty-one days after the fire in the care of an uncle, Victor Clare. There was an address, so faded it couldn't be read. The child's medical record was stored somewhere else, so I didn't bother looking for it. Next stop: Southern Bell.

There were three Clares in the '32 telephone directory. V. E. Clare lived at 6906 Monessen. I looked up the street on a city map.

On my way to Victor Clare's address I went by the block where the tailor Kennedy had been burned out. Most of an old neighborhood shopping center had been razed in favor of modern apartments. There was a drive-in near the former location of the shop, half a block of asphalt chopped up into rectangles by yellow guide lines for parking, with a circular barbecue shack in the center. On a hot night you could probably smell the place half a mile downwind. Girl carhops in sandals, chartreuse Bermudas and perky little overseas caps leaned into the shade afforded by a tired awning and lifted one foot and then the other away from the slow sizzle of the asphalt. So that was progress. I drove on.

The Monessen address was a narrow pink stucco apartment house with two stories of screened porches across the front supported by flaked white columns. The place looked like last year's birthday cake. I parked in front and went up to the door. There was a small bicycle parked in the middle of the yellow lawn and a '49 Ford halfway down the drive that ended in a sagging garage at the rear of the place. I went inside. There was a door to the left in the small foyer and a flight of stairs with worn rubber matting that led steeply to the second floor. Two mailboxes gave me the names Matlock and Torrance. No Clare.

I looked up the steps and sighed. Halfway up there was a shallow depression in the plaster, as if the upstairs tenant paused in his journey up the steps each evening to beat his head against the wall. I reached out and touched the doorbell button of the downstairs apartment.

The door was opened presently by a girl about five feet tall wearing pale blue jeans and a man's handkerchief tied around her forehead. She held an infant in one small arm. She couldn't have been more than nineteen.

She smiled up at me. "Yes?"

"Mrs. Matlock?"

"Ye-es." She sort of blushed at the thought that she was Mrs. Matlock.

"I'm trying to find out about a man who used to live here. A Mr. Clare. It was about twenty-five years ago."

Mrs. Matlock frowned slightly. "I'm afraid I wouldn't be much help. I wasn't even born then."

"Have you lived here long?"

"Oh, no. About a year."

"Do you remember who had the apartment before you?"

"Some people named Gruen. Like the watch. They lived here since before the Second World War."

"I see. Uh—the people upstairs. Torrance? Do you know how long they've—"

The baby gurgled comfortably. Mrs. Matlock stood patiently, holding the weight of him on one hip. "They've only lived here about four months. Before then Frank's— Mr. Matlock's—grandmother lived alone upstairs. She lived here for a long time."

"Do you know where I might get in touch with Mrs. Matlock?"

"Oh, you couldn't. I mean, she died. About six months ago. Ye gads, the phone. I'll get rid of whoever it is." She thrust the baby at me. "Here, you hold—do you know how to hold?"

I took the baby and showed her I knew how to hold. She scampered off to the phone. She was back in a minute. "Thanks, I'll take him. C'mon, Stevie." She heaved him gently to her shoulder. "Woof, he's getting heavy," she said. "You see, Frank and I own the apartment. His grandmother gave it to us when we got married. Said we'd need a place, we were just starting out, and she just wanted a roof over her head. A place to sit until she died, she used to say. She was kind of funny. Then she did die. After that we let the Torrances move in. They're about our age. We play bridge every Wednesday." She looked at me expectantly.

"I—thank you for giving me so much of your time, Mrs. Matlock."

"That's all right. You didn't tell me your name."

"Mallory. Pete Mallory."

"I'm sorry I couldn't help you, Mr. Mallory."

I said goodbye and helped her shut the door. Outside I took out my handkerchief and wiped my face. The rest of the block consisted of small houses, except for a used-furniture store toward the Kelvin Boulevard intersection and a drugstore across the street from that.

I tried the house next door on the right. On the porch two small boys were drawing on the floor with chalk. A dog bared his teeth at me and backed under a chair at the same time. A plump white-haired woman was using a vacuum cleaner in the living room. Without turning off the vacuum or stopping work, she put across to me that she had never heard of Victor Clare.

Across the street a thin tired-looking man sat on the porch, his long brown hair waving in the stream of air from a fan about a foot from his face. He was reading a racing sheet and making marks in some kind of personal code on a pad of scratch paper. He gave me the time it took him to light a fresh cigarette. He managed to light it and keep a hand over the scratch pad at the same time. It was quite a feat.

He didn't know Victor Clare. His wife didn't know Victor Clare. They had lived in the house about ten years.

He didn't remember the name of the man they had bought the house from. I wouldn't want him to look it up, would I? I told him not to bother.

It took me thirty minutes to get the same answer at the other houses on the street. By that time all the neighbors had an eye on me as I walked along the street. To give them time to forget it and to make sure I didn't miss any bets, I went to the used-furniture store.

A little bell above the door went off when I shoved it open. It was hot inside. The air smelled as if no one had been breathing it lately. There was a small path across the scuffed floor to a pair of curtains with a two-inch space between them. The rest of the floor was crowded with indifferent furniture.

"You wanted to buy something?" a tough female voice said from beyond the curtains.

"I don't know," I said. "I wanted to talk to someone."

"Come on back," the voice invited.

It was even hotter at the back of the store. Part of the floor was concrete and there was a small brick oven against one wall. Tall thin windows filtered light through the dirty crusty glass. There were shelves everywhere, stacked with hundreds of little clay figures of soldiers, children dressed in costumes from a dozen countries, animals, characters from fairy tales. On a large table about three and a half feet high were boxes of modeling clay, cans of paint and glazing compound, stacks of books and magazines, tools to aid in shaping the figures. Two long-necked lamps at each end of the table provided most of the light.

A large fat woman with olive skin and bluish gray hair neatly waved on her round skull worked at the table, her fingers squeezing and kneading clay. She wore a black dress buttoned close to her chin and spreading amply over her length of fat, ending a few inches above her ankles. She had sharp eyes behind black-rimmed glasses, and jabbed them at me when I came through the curtains. I saw that she had been watching the store through the curtains with the aid of a small mirror on the table. A huge fan on the floor a dozen feet behind her didn't disturb the steamy air much. I was sweating before I'd taken half a dozen steps. Apparently she was firing some of the figures in the oven.

"What could I do for you?" she said, her fingers never stopping their work.

The heat made me feel weak in the stomach. "I've been looking for a man named Victor Clare. He used to live down the street, at Sixty-nine-o-six, but nobody there has heard of him."

"What do you want with him?"

I named a fictitious lawyer that I was representing. "He's come into a little money. We'd like to find him and make the disposition."

"He died," she said. "Heart attack. About Thirty-three, it was."

"I'm sorry to hear it," I said. I hesitated. "There was a little girl who lived with him. Carla Kennedy. He took care of her after her parents were killed in a fire."

Her fingers continued to work at the clay until a figure began to emerge. I was beginning to think she hadn't understood me.

"I remember the child," she said then. "I remember when she came to live with him. He was her uncle, I believe."

"What did the girl look like?"

She took off her glasses, wiped them on a handkerchief. "What insurance company did you say you were with?"

"Lawyer," I corrected. She wasn't believing a word of it.

"She was a very pretty child," the woman said. "I remember that."

"Do you remember what color hair she had?"

"I never knew. Most of it was burned off. Sort of brownish, I think. She didn't live in the neighborhood long, after her uncle died."

Her busy fingers finished the rough outline of her current figurine. She held it up for me. "There. How's that?"

"Fine. What happened to the girl after that?"

She shook her head. "I couldn't say." She put down the clay, scraped bits of it from her hands with a thin, filelike blade. She stood up, holding on to the table for support. She wasn't much taller standing up. She went to a shelf nearby and took down one of the figures.

"I have one here I think you'd like," she said, bringing it with her and lifting it toward me. It was a little Southern girl in a bell-shaped hoop skirt. I turned the glazed statuette in my hands, looking at it from all angles. "What's the price?"

"Twenty dollars." Her sharp eyes were almost ashamed.

I looked around the dreary little store. "That's pretty steep. What goes with the figure for the twenty dollars?"

"I think I can find out where Carla Kennedy is for you." Her eyes prodded me. "I don't get around so good any more. It'll take a little time."

"How much time?"

She dug around in a pocket of the shapeless black dress, and her fingers came out holding a scrap of paper. She had to sit down from the effort of her search. She held out the paper to me. There was a phone number written on it.

"Call me tomorrow night about seven. If the girl's still in town I'll get in touch with her."

"Twenty dollars," I said sorrowfully.

"Well," she said defensively, looking at the statuette, "I'm probably saving you a lot of time."

I nodded and reached into my hip pocket for my wallet.

Chapter Eleven

I memorized the phone number, Seminole 4-3278, as I walked slowly back to where I had parked the Buick earlier that morning. It was close to noon. I sidestepped a small boy wheeling a tricycle around the sidewalk, opened the door and slid into the car. The boy stopped pedaling and watched me from the sidewalk with round serious eyes.

I wadded up the slip of paper and put it in the ashtray, got out the key and stuck it in the ignition.

"Did he fix yoah cah?" the boy said suddenly in a shrill voice. It startled me.

"What?"

He stared at me, mouth open. His face needed washing. "Da man fix yoah cah," he said clearly.

"This car?"

He nodded, rode the tricycle in a furious circle, stopped, stared at me again.

"When?"

He pointed up the street. "Jus' left."

I looked at the key in the ignition, frowned at it. I withdrew it carefully and put it in my pocket, then got out of the Buick, walked around it and lifted the hood. In a minute or so I found the gimmick, unwired it from the starter and pulled it tenderly away from the motor. Three sticks of dynamite wired together composed the guts of the homemade starter bomb. If I had turned the key in the ignition, the Buick would have looked as though it had been dropped into the middle of the street from an airplane. What I would have looked like was too sickening to think about.

I put the thing in the trunk, wrapping it in an old inner tube and sticking it into a corner where it wouldn't bounce around. The little boy was still close by. He had saved his own life as well as mine by speaking out. He had a pleased smile on his face.

"He fix yoah cah."

"He sure did," I said. I had to sit down. I opened the door of the Buick next to the sidewalk and sat inside, my feet on the pavement.

"Come here a minute, son," I said.

He backpedaled cautiously. "Ma said not to."

"Okay, then. Stay there. Did you watch this man fix my car?" He nodded.

"What did he look like? Was he as big as I am?" He nodded again.

"Bigger?" He looked uncertain.

"Came in a car?" Nod.

"Was it a big car, like this one?" Not sure.

"What color?" Blue.

"What was he wearing? Like I've got on, a suit?"

He studied this. "Ov'alls," he said.

Overalls. I tried to think what else I could ask him that he might have paid attention to. License number? Ha-ha. I was too upset to think it through. I wanted to get in the car and drive it right back to Orange Bay. A sudden thought came to me.

"Did he have on a hat? A blue hat?" The head went from side to side, slowly. Well, that was crazy, anyway.

Down the street a woman yelled hoarsely, "Ronniieeee!" We both jumped. He looked around, aimed the tricycle in that direction and pedaled off.

That left me alone on the lazy noon street. A breath of air touched my hot forehead. I wondered if any of the neighbors had noticed the phony mechanic doctoring the Buick, decided it wasn't worth asking. I got under the wheel, put the key in the ignition gingerly and winced when I turned it, forgetting to step on the gas.

"Oh, Elaine," I said under my breath. "Elaine, Elaine, Elaine." I drove away from there. Ten minutes later I felt the first satisfying edge of anger and my stomach had stopped jumping. I parked in front of a drugstore. I had a very vague idea and nothing else to do but track it down.

I found the number I wanted and a fresh young voice answered right away. "Stan's Restaurant." I asked her where Stan was. She didn't know. He usually came in for lunch but today he must have gone home to eat. I asked where home was. "I can't give out that information," she said coldly. I hung up.

Just for the hell of it I looked through the phone book and there it was. Maxine, Stanley, 1901 Jacaranda. I went outside to the Buick, dug out the city map again and found Jacaranda. It was in the Lake Alena section, a block from the golf course that rimmed the west side of the lake.

In fifteen minutes I was there. It was a nice two-story house of peach-colored stucco, with a little Mexican balcony above the front entrance, and a big side porch.

There was no car parked in front and I didn't see a drive, so I decided the garage could be reached only from the rear. I rang the doorbell.

"You want something?" a soft voice said behind me.

I turned and looked at a big Negro with elegantly graying hair and magnificent shoulders. He was wearing levis, a T shirt and a bandana around his throat. He carried a pair of hedge clippers.

"I was looking for Stan," I said pleasantly.

The hedge clippers went *chop-chop.* "He's not here," he said in an unfriendly tone.

"When would he be likely to get here?"

"I wouldn't know that," the man said. "I just work here."

The front door opened. I looked at a girl in red toreador pants and a bare-midriff blouse. She had lots of soft dark-red hair with streaks in it like hot flame, high cheekbones, cozy blue eyes. She had a near-perfect figure and the clothing she liked made you instantly familiar with every good line of it. Her breasts were almost outsized. She stood with one hand on a stuck-out hip, the other on the doorframe.

"Hello," she said. She looked past me at the gardener. "Who's this, Bradley?"

"I don't know, ma'am," he said in his dignified voice. "He was looking for Mr. Maxine."

She looked at me. "Stan's not here. He was, but he left just a few minutes ago." She smiled. "Could I help?"

"I don't—"

"Come on in anyway," she invited, turning to let me see the profile. She stood straight, belly flattened a little too much, as if she were holding it in. I could see the rounded edge of her rib cage.

I went past her into the house. It was very cool inside. The living room was wide and deep and shady, decorated and planned by an expert to seem as casual as a chew of tobacco. There was a patio beyond wide French doors, with gaudy lawn furniture.

"I'm Gerry," she said, sitting on the edge of the sofa. She was barefoot. "Are you a friend of Stan's?"

"Yes. Are you?"

That got her. She laughed charmingly, a laugh that put dimples at the corners of her mouth. "I sure am," she said.

A sudden gash of sound startled me. It was a booming bass voice rolling out a piece of something from an opera. The singing was excellent, though loud enough to wrinkle glass. It ended as abruptly as it had begun. I looked around in bewilderment.

"What was that?"

Gerry shrugged. "Bradley. You saw him outside. He's going to be an opera singer."

"What does he do around here?"

"Oh, he works for Stan. He's sort of a gardener and chauffeur, and he keeps an eye on the place. Spends most of his spare time taking singing lessons. He breaks out like that all the time. I've got used to it. The neighbors complain, though. The people next door moved away because their cocker spaniel went around shaking all the time and wouldn't eat."

"Could you tell me where I might find Stan?" I asked her.

She tossed her head, putting fingers to her hair. She slid a look at me I wasn't supposed to see. It totaled me up like an adding machine.

"I suppose he went back to the office. He's president of Marlin Linen Supply Company. You didn't tell me your name."

"His name's Pete Mallory," Stan Maxine said.

Neither of us started guiltily. Maxine was standing in the doorway to the dining room looking at us. Gerry glanced at him casually.

"I thought you were gone, Stan."

Stan mopped his misting dark face with a pink handkerchief. He wore a cream-colored suit, dull orange dress shirt with a black tie, and black suede shoes. His hair was tumbling on his forehead and he waved it back into place with fingers that trembled slightly.

"I, ah, I forgot my stomach medicine, sweetie," he said. His moist, moody eyes kept swinging back to me. There were acne scars on either cheek, and the knife scar at one corner of his mouth held his lips slightly apart and got in the way of his speech when he talked rapidly, which was most of the time. There was a congested look on his face as he suppressed a stomach rumble.

"It's probably upstairs," Gerry offered, swinging one small foot briskly as she sat on the arm of the sofa.

"Yeah," Stan said. "Probably. Listen, honey, would you mind going into the kitchen and maybe stick the dishes in the washer while Mallory and I talk private?"

Gerry grimaced unhappily.

"Just for a minute or two, honey," Stan coaxed. She picked up a pair of slip-on shoes and walked slowly toward the dining room. When she was close to Maxine she looked back at me and a smile touched one corner of her mouth. Maxine's finger flexed, but he continued to look at her fondly. When she had shut the door to the dining room he took three big strides toward the sofa, his face pinched with fury, snatched up a big square pillow, turned and flung it at the closed door.

"I'm gonna catch you one of these days, you little tramp!" he said fiercely under his breath. I didn't quite smile at him. Stan always made the slightest movement seem incredibly difficult to achieve, throwing his whole body into a wink, a word, a gesture. I've never seen him still for longer than half a minute.

"She's cute as a speckled pup," I said. "When did you marry her?"

"She's not my wife," he said, turning his constant sneer on me. His hair had fallen out of place again and he pushed it violently off his forehead. Since I had known him he had shaved his sideburns. It was an improvement, but Stan needed lots more of them. His teeth gleamed inside the slight gap between his lips.

He looked around the living room, then took a prescription bottle from his coat pocket, uncapped it, sipped some of the rich creamy liquid. He looked like it hurt him to drink it. When he had had enough he replaced the lid, dropped the medicine into his pocket.

"About eighteen, isn't she?" I said. From what I'd seen of Gerry she could be that young, or she could be ten years older. It was hard to tell.

"That's none of your goddam business. Gerry just looks young. She's been around." He eyed me narrowly. "I thought I'd never have to look at you again," he said. "What did you come back for, Pete?"

"Pick out a reason you like," I told him, wondering if he'd heard about the mail Macy had been getting.

"I don't like none of 'em." He walked around the sofa twice, then sat down, his anxious fingers finding a cigarette to play with. "You got a reason for coming here?"

"I want to know which one of your boys is a chunky

little customer with a sky blue hat and a white band."

He put the cigarette in a corner of his mouth. "Why?"

"I ran into a shotgun ambush last night on my way into town. He was the triggerman. An hour ago somebody rigged a bomb in my car. There was enough dynamite hooked up to the starter to blast me to Key West. It may or may not have been the same lad. When I find him I'm going to blow his face right out from under that beautiful hat."

Stan put his head back and laughed. I could see gold in his teeth. "He's not mine. I never knew you were coming. My boys wouldn't goof the job twice, either."

I reached down and jerked him off the sofa by the front of his coat. He swung a wild fist at me. I stepped out of the way of it and grinned at him. His hands patted the rumpled coat. I had an eye cocked for a gun but apparently he didn't carry one. His bad skin reddened. He stuck out a trembling finger at me.

"You don't shake me up no more, Pete," he spit out, forgetting the good English in his haste. "I'm big now, Pete. I snap my fingers, I got two-three guys to blow your gut out. Sure, I know why you're back. But you came too late. Macy's on his way out. I'm the new man in town. You stay away from me or maybe I will arrange a party for you. Don't mess with me." His eyes were dull with hate. He jerked a thumb at the closed door to the dining room. "Don't mess around her!"

I looked at him until I thought he might try to slug me again. Then I walked toward the front door. I went up the two steps into the hall, then looked back at him. He had the pink handkerchief out again.

"Maybe you're right," I said casually. "Maybe Macy's

through. But like you said—I'm back." I was just popping off. But his shoulders hunched and he looked at me with one glassy eye. There was murder in it. The other was almost shut in rage. He drew back a little and his mouth opened and his neck swelled.

I opened the door and went outside, but not before I heard him shriek childishly, "I hate your goddam *guuuuuts*, Pete!"

Chapter Twelve

Three blocks down the street I saw a familiar figure in red pants hiking briskly along. When she heard the Buick approach she turned and gave me the thumb expectantly. So I pulled over and she hopped in.

"I thought you were doing the dishes," I said.

She took a comb from her purse and went to work tidying her hair. "No. I went upstairs and turned on the shower a little bit. Stan'll think I'm taking a bath and when I don't answer he'll think I'm sulking. Then he'll go on back to work." The comb made shushing sounds in her thick hair. "I thought you all would be talking a while longer. Stan might have caught me."

Gerry put the comb away and rooted around for a lipstick. She adjusted the rearview mirror so she could see herself in it. "Mind if I borrow this?"

"What's Stan going to say when he finds you're gone?"

She rolled her eyes. "He'll raise the roof. But I know how to handle him…most of the time," she added thoughtfully. She touched up her lips with a shade that might have been called Carnal Red. "I wouldn't usually run out like this unless Stan said I could, but it's kind of important." She patted the full lips with a Kleenex. "He won't give me a car. He's afraid I've got other boyfriends."

"Don't you?"

She gave me a cautious look. "No. Not exactly. I've got a friend…but he's not exactly a boy. He's older. You going downtown?" I nodded. She settled back after turning on the radio.

"Besides," she said, "Stan's got other girls. I know. I've seen one of them. I was supposed to be upstairs in bed. They were on the sofa. It was kind of dark. She was a blonde. I don't like blondes."

"You go to school?"

This tickled her. "Me?"

"How old are you?"

"Old enough," she said wisely. She looked at me closely, as if she wasn't quite happy riding with me any more.

"Where are you going?" I asked her.

"Oh, any place downtown will be fine. I'm going to the Coral Gardens Hotel—that's over on the beach. But I can catch a bus or something."

"In those pants," I said, "you could catch anything."

"Huh?"

"As a matter of fact, I was going that way myself," I said, and shut up.

At the Coral Gardens Hotel I put the Buick in a no-parking zone square in front of the canopy. The Coral Gardens was a modest seven-story building, its yellow color mellowed and softened by the salt wind off the Atlantic that crept to the back doorstep like a great patient beast.

Once the Coral Gardens had been a favorite of migrating and vacationing hoods from the North, but newer and more splendid places with names like *Cote d'Or* and *Chateau Castile* had lured the trade away. A few old-timers, friends of Macy, still settled there during the winter, but, on the whole, it had turned respectable.

Gerry waited patiently for me to come around and

open the door for her. "You busy right now?" she asked, stepping out of the Buick.

"No, I don't think so."

She took me by the hand. "I want to show you something," she said urgently, and took me around to the back of the hotel, down a flight of steps to the damp smelly basement. There were dressing stalls for swimmers down here and puddles of water on the concrete floor. A window fan roared and rattled, and an old man wearing a T shirt stenciled *Coral Gardens Hotel* waited patiently for the puddles to dry so he could put away the mop he was leaning on.

We went into a large room near the steps to the lobby upstairs. Here the air was cleaner and drier and sunlight touched all corners through two big windows. It seemed to be some kind of art studio. There was a raised platform against the wall under the windows and behind it was an old tarpaulin backdrop. Finished canvases leaned against the walls. Tubes of oils and brushes were scattered on a table convenient to an easel. There were a couple of sofas for lounging or other basic pleasures.

Gerry pointed to a partially completed portrait on the easel. "Owen's painting a picture of me," she said proudly.

I looked at it closely. She was posed astraddle a straight-back chair, one cheek resting on her crossed forearms. The expression on her face was stiff and lifeless. The rest of her nude body was very well done. Breasts jutted high, and the contours of stomach and abdomen were properly shadowed. Owen had duplicated skin tone well, but he was having some trouble getting the shade he wanted for her hair.

"Don't touch it," Gerry warned. "Owen's not through. It's not dry yet." She looked at me for approval. "It's good, isn't it?" I said it was good. She walked around the studio, looking at other paintings, her hips rolling neatly in the tight toreador pants. "He's got talent," she said. "Owen's really got talent."

I wondered what Maxine would do if he knew Owen Barr was entertaining his girlfriend. I could imagine.

I told her I had things to do. She made no move to go with me. I went up the stairs and met Owen Barr walking across the lobby. He had come out of the package store and carried a wrapped bottle under his arm. He seemed surprised to find me there. He wore an unpressed gray jacket and baggy dark green slacks.

"Hello, Mallory," he said, frowning past me at the basement. When I nodded he clutched the bottle more tightly and went around me, his eyes sulky.

I got a room and key at the desk and went back downstairs. The door to the studio was closed, but it wasn't much of a door. With my ear against it I could hear very well.

"Are you going to paint this afternoon?" Gerry said.

"I don't know. Sick of it. Where's a glass?"

"Over there. It's sure beginning to look like me."

"The tits look like you. The rest—I can't seem to get the face right. Oh, the hell with it! You want a drink?"

"No. Is something wrong?"

"Everything's always wrong. Come on and sit down."

"When do you think you'll finish it?"

"I don't know. Maybe I won't finish it. What's the use? I'm no damn good."

"You *are* good!"

"No damn good. Aw, baby, don't do that. I don't feel like it."

"I wish you wouldn't drink so much. I thought you were going to paint today. I sneaked out of the house—"

"Just leave me alone. I don't feel like listening. Maybe Macy's right. Maybe it is just junk. I'm no damn good."

"Don't feel that way."

"I'm glad somebody is trying to kill him. Really glad. I hope the bastard gets it good. All my life he's ordered me around. Just a stinking big shot. Order me around. I never had a real chance. Nobody ever paid any attention to me, because of goddam Macy. I...I..."

"Owen!"

"You like me, don't you, baby? Pretty Gerry—like me, don't you?"

"Sure I do, Owen. And you know I don't like Macy any better than you do. Not after he treated me the way he did."

"The stinking big shot. You do this, Owen. You do that, Owen. I'm no goddam dog. I got feelings like anybody else. I never had a real chance....Where'd I put that bottle? You'll stay with me, won't you, Gerry? Let me have another drink, and then we'll look at the painting. I want to sketch your face, and maybe I can get it right— you'll stick around, honey?"

I looked down the hall, saw the shower-room attendant creaking toward me with the mop over his shoulder. I took my ear away from the door and Owen's vocal pangs of misery and went upstairs, wondering why Maxine's girl should hate Macy Barr.

There was no point in bothering with Gerry any longer; I didn't want to stay sidetracked. I had to find out who was so persistently trying to knock me off. And I knew just the man to ask about it, although all I had to go on was a sketchy description and a pale blue hat with a light-colored band.

It wouldn't be easy. In six years sources of information that I had once depended upon would be dried up. There would be new contacts, new people to see. But at least I had an idea where to start.

Chapter Thirteen

The Rendezvous was a charming basement beer hall near the ship channel. It stank of spilled brew, dirty clothing and the elusive scent of rare sin. The rest of the building was a honeycomb of rooms for furtive meetings, the exchange of smuggled goods, the viewing of strange sex acts. I had been there often in my fledgling days with Macy.

I went down dirty littered steps to a little concrete-paved area that looked like the drunk tank in a jail. There was a man in one corner, huddled away from the touch of sun on the floor. The drain was layered with filth. I stepped over it, holding my breath, went through old-fashioned swinging doors and down two steps to get to The Rendezvous. It hadn't changed much. They still didn't believe in lights. The floor was the same buckled linoleum, and the walls were as damp as ever. The customers might have been the same. I didn't know. I couldn't see their faces. At The Rendezvous there are few faces, few names to be remembered. They had a jukebox but it wasn't working. The only sounds were the buzz of a fly, the slow swing of a fan, the broken garble of a man talking to himself in one of the secluded corners.

A few eyes looked at me as I walked across linoleum hills and sat down at a table. I moved the chair a little so I had the wall at my back. I did it without thinking about it. I had learned that precaution a long time ago in The Rendezvous.

The bartender saw that I was too well dressed to be on a casual drinking tour. He put a towel over one arm, shuffled around the bar and came suspiciously toward me. His right side seemed frozen. The shoulder was down and he dragged that leg with an effort. He wasn't old. His face had a square sullen look.

"What do you want?" he said.

"Whisky." I looked around. A woman sitting at a table near the door was combing stringy hair and looking at me expectantly. She had been playing some kind of game with bottle caps when I came in. I let the bartender know I was looking at her.

"Make it two," I said.

"Ah," he grunted. It had satisfied him to know what I had in mind. Half of him dragged the other half back to the bar.

She walked over to me with too much hip swing. She wore a cheap flower-print cotton dress that ended a couple of inches below her knees. She sat down next to me, smiled a little. She had heavy lips and a chin that sagged. Flesh shook on the bones of her upper arms when she moved them.

I smiled back. "Hot day," I said.

"Yeah." She smoothed hair on top of her head with chubby fingers. The hair looked as if it had been dyed with coffee. "That's why I like to sit in here on days like this. Too hot to go out." Her eyes were busy, deciding how much I was worth.

"I bought you a drink," I said, trying to seem pleasantly nervous. "I thought you might like one."

"Well, thanks." We were good buddies. She grabbed hers off the tray while the bartender was still approaching the table. I took the other glass and paid him. I didn't touch mine. She drank hers with relish, the throat muscles pulling greedily.

"Say," she said, swinging the glass down. "That's good. Good as gold." She licked her lips.

I put my own down, trying to look as if I had enjoyed it. "Yeah," I said solemnly. "It's good to taste liquor again."

Her eyes went appraisingly over my suit. She reached out and handled the sleeve. "That's a pretty good suit," she said wittily.

I kept looking at her as if she were the closest thing to an angel I had seen yet. I hoped my look was full of lust. "They gave it to me when I got out," I said.

She nodded. "Thought I recognized the cut of it. Prison goods." She crossed her legs, because it was about that time in the script—the script she had written for herself a long time ago. Her hips pushed tightly against the thin dress. I looked where I was supposed to look.

"How long were you in?" she said.

"Five years."

"That's too bad," she said sympathetically. "Five years in the can ain't no fun. No liquor. No women." She gave me a long look. "Say," she said, "I got half a bottle in my room. I mean, it's goin' to waste, I don't like to drink alone. You and me could have a pull at it. I mean, since you just got out and all—"

"I'd like that," I said. "Where's your room?"

She nodded. "Up the stairs back there. It's not a very fancy place. Just a place to lay my head." She giggled. We got up together. She took my hand and led me past the bartender. He didn't look at us.

Her hand felt damp and slightly greasy. She held

tightly to me, almost pulling me up the narrow stairway. I stopped when we went through the door into her room. A man was sitting at a table in the center of the floor, his face on the yellowing cloth. He was snoring his head off. There was a jug of cheap wine near him. I could smell it throughout the room.

"Don't mind him," she said. "He'll sleep for hours." She released my hand, went to the bed, lifted a thin, stained mattress, pulled a flat bottle of whisky from under it.

"Here we are, honey," she said gaily, holding the bottle high. She pitched it at me. "Catch. Glasses over there on the dresser."

I turned away and set the bottle on the dresser. The hot room smelled vaguely like a whore-house scrub room. There was a toilet in one corner that bubbled constantly.

I heard her unzipping the dress and turned around. She wiggled out of it, kicked it away with a heavy flat foot. She wore no underwear. Her breasts sagged over her belly. The nipples pointed almost straight down.

"After you've had some of that you can have some of this," she said, pointing. "But only the booze is free, baby."

I took out my wallet, peeled off a five-dollar bill. I put the wallet back. Her eyes were bright. "We could have a real party," she said, the words oozing out. "Maybe some harder stuff than whisky. Lots harder."

"What name you go by?"

"Gretchen. Just call me Gretchen, darlin'. Let's have that drink."

"No, thanks. The five only buys one thing."

She stopped advancing toward me. "What's that, darlin'? I don't go in for none of these tricks—"

"I just want to know where Rose is. That's what I get for the five."

She frowned. "Rose?"

"She used to work here. About five years ago. For all I know she's still here."

I had her puzzled. "She did work here. She ain't here now. She—"

I found myself listening with part of my mind for a sound that wasn't there any more. I turned toward the table as the man who had been sitting there leaped at me. Surprise was all he had. When I turned I took that away from him and all that was left was a big double-edged knife and no technique. He slashed at me with the blade from a place behind his ear. I got an arm up to block his try, then hammered him in the gut. He hit the floor on his back. I stepped on his wrist with one foot, kicked the knife out of his hand with the other. I kept my foot on the wrist and looked at him while he went about learning how to breathe again. He was dark and had a thick mustache.

"Who are you?" the naked woman said shrilly. "What d'you want?"

I told her to shut up. I hauled the guy off his back and hit him in the mouth. He stumbled back against the table, then dived for his knife. I was already there. I picked it up. The blade was about a mile long, and the handle was wrapped with tape. There was dried blood on the tape. The blade looked as if it had been sharpened many times, done much work.

I picked him up again and jammed him against the wall and put the edge of the blade under his chin. He sweated wine from every pore. He chewed me out in thick jumbled Spanish.

"What was this supposed to be?" I said. "Your afternoon workout?"

"Ain't no goddam cop gonna come around here actin' wise," he said.

"What do you care how she earns her money? What are you to her, anyway?"

"Anything I want to be, buster," he said.

I glanced back over my shoulder. The woman was wearily putting on her dress again. This whole bit didn't interest her.

"Suppose you tell me where I can find Rose?"

"Suppose you—" he said.

"You gonna cut his throat or not?" the woman said in a hard voice.

"I'm working up to it," I said.

"You won't get nothin' from him," she said with a little rattling laugh. "He ain't afraid of nothin'. Cut his throat and he'll kick your ass off while he's bleeding to death."

"Isn't that lovely?" I said. She was probably right.

"I don't want you to have to maul him," she said. "Rose lives with a guy now."

"Where?"

"Two months ago it was a walkup over on Chambliss. Twenty-five-ten Chambliss. Today it might be somewhere else."

I pounded the guy's head against the wall and let him go. He staggered to the table and leaned hard on it. There was blood on his lips.

I gave the woman the five dollars. She took it and held

it while she zipped the dress. The guy straightened up, looked at me, looked at the five dollars. He walked over to her, stumbling slightly. He took the five dollars and belted her across the face. They glared at each other.

"Nex' time you don't go shooting your mouth off," he said, breathing hard. She didn't say anything. Her cheeks had flushed red.

"I'll leave your knife downstairs with the bartender," I said. "Maybe you better go down to the juvenile hall and get some kid to show you how to use it before you wave it around again."

I went downstairs and handed the knife to the bartender. He looked it over and looked at me. I walked on out. I was happy to be leaving.

The address on Chambliss turned out to be an old brick apartment building in a mixed neighborhood just a couple of blocks from a Negro slum. The only whites in the neighborhood were those who couldn't afford to move somewhere else, and the liquor-store owners.

On the front porch an aging woman with skin that looked as if it were stuck to her face with rubber cement told me that a woman named Rose lived on the third floor. She told me to use the back stairs.

I walked through the narrow concrete-paved areaway between two buildings. Small children were playing on the entire length of it, and in the barren back yard. They climbed on the shed roof and crawled behind the row of garbage cans and waded in the small pools of muddy water. Older children sat on the steps and looked at me with dull, arrogant eyes as I brushed by them.

It was a long climb to the third floor. I stopped a couple of times on the landings, then brushed by lines hung with sodden wash and climbed on until I came to the right door.

I could see the woman through an open kitchen window. She was washing dishes in a pan on the sink and having a hard time of it. Her lips were pursed in concentration. She turned at the sound of my fist against the door, dried her hand on an apron and came to the door.

She had waxy yellow hair and tight good skin that wouldn't wrinkle no matter what her age. She might have been forty, but I couldn't be sure. Her hair was combed straight back and tied with a piece of faded purple ribbon.

"Rose?" I said.

"Yes?" She bent quickly to push a puppy back into the kitchen, with her one hand. When I knew her she had both arms. Now the left one was cut off below the shoulder, and the short sleeve of the dress she wore was tied down over the stump.

"My name's Pete Mallory. I used to know you about six years ago, when you were at The Rendezvous."

Mention of The Rendezvous caused her to frown. She tugged a little at the apron with her hand. "I don't believe I remember you. At The Rendezvous—" She shrugged. Her mouth had a slightly bitter twist to it.

"I know," I said. The puppy was trying to squirm outside again and this time she held him back with a small foot. "You see, I'm looking for a man. I thought if I could find the Preacher or someone like that, he could help me." The Preacher was sort of a code name for a man who had sold information about anything and everything.

She shook her head. "The Preacher's dead. He died about five years ago."

"Oh. I guess that had to happen," I said.

"He wasn't killed. He had a heart attack. I'm afraid I can't help you. I left The Rendezvous months ago." She looked without meaning to at the tied-off sleeve.

"I thought maybe you knew someone like The Preacher who could tell me what I need to know."

"No. No." She shook her head emphatically. But she kept looking at me as if her memory were beginning to thaw a little. "I don't know any man like that any more. I haven't known any since I left The Rendezvous."

She tried to close the door. But I was leaning against the jamb and she couldn't push it past me. "Are you sure you don't remember me?" I said.

Little paths of perspiration covered her face. "No," she breathed. "No, I don't. Please go away."

"I saved your life once," I said quietly. "I kept a drunk from tearing your throat out with a broken bottle. You probably don't remember, because you were drunk, too. But I had to kick in a door to get at him. I've got a little scar from that on my hand, where a splinter of wood gouged me." I looked at the hand. "You can't see it so good any more," I added.

Her eyes were large and she looked a little frightened. "I don't believe you. Get out of the door and go away and leave me be."

"You've got a scar, too, where the bottle raked you as he fell. There should be a scar, anyway, right near your hip. It was a deep cut."

She tottered back a couple of steps, her eyes on my face. "I...I have that scar," she said.

I pushed the door open and came inside. I stopped and scooped up the puppy. He squirmed in my hands and chewed at the cuff of my coat.

"Now *I* need help, Rose," I said.

"Don't expect me to be able to help you," she said. She leaned against a table covered with a red-and-white checkered cloth. "I don't know anything now. Once I gave information." She put the hand to her face. There was a slight look of shock in her eyes. "And once I had none to give." Her eyes ranged from me to the floor and then to the sink, like wild things. "That time I had none to give, they thought I was lying. They were big men. Foreign. They didn't care that I was a woman. They had my arm." Her eyes went to the sleeve and were full of horror that hadn't diminished with the passing of time. "They twisted it. And...twisted it—"

"That's enough," I said.

Her lips were apart. They were dry lips, with no touch of red. "Now you want information and I don't have any to give. I don't know anything."

I put the puppy down before he could ruin my sleeve. "I'll go," I said. "I'm sorry for—bothering you."

"Wait." She straightened up from the table, swallowed hard. "It was a worthless life," she said. "But you saved it. You must have, or you wouldn't know about the scar. Now I've got a good man. A good man to make something of the worthless life."

She walked to the sink with quick steps, filled a glass with water. "This man you want—what is he?"

"A hired killer, I think."

She nodded, once. "Then you speak to Dave. Dave might be able to help you."

"Who is Dave?"

She turned from the sink after drinking. Her eyes were full of fierce hate and woman's tenderness and you could see them both at the same time. "He was a detective with the police. He was a good detective, until they took his badge. He's in the bedroom. Asleep. I'll go talk to him. You sit down, please. Would you like some cookies?"

"No, thank you. I'll just wait."

I watched her leave the kitchen. Her figure was good, even after years of abuse at The Rendezvous and other such places. She talked with a certain dignity that hinted at the rare fine qualities of this former gutter orphan.

I gave the pup a hard time with my foot, rolling him over on the floor when he tried to chew my toe off. He growled and attacked, swinging furry stiff paws at the shoe. He had a great time.

Finally she came back. "Dave said he'll see you," she said, and told me how to find him. She remained in the kitchen.

The man called Dave sat on the edge of a big double bed in the bedroom. He rubbed at crisp black hair that showed spikes of white. There were smudges under his eyes and his skin was pale, as if he had spent a lot of time indoors. He wore shorts and an undershirt that was soaked with perspiration. He wasn't more than five feet seven, but he must have weighed close to 175 pounds. He had probably been a rough cop. Vice-squad material.

"Come on in," he growled, holding his head. A gun and holster hung on a high-backed rocking chair near the bed. There was a bottle of whisky on a solid little table within reaching distance.

"Rose said I got to help you, if I can," he said, not happy about the idea. He didn't look at me for more than two seconds. The eyes were sharp and petulant. He grabbed the bottle and glass and poured himself one.

"Sit down. Drink?"

"No, thanks." I sat on the edge of the rocker. There was a badge pinned to the worn leather of the holster. He had been a sergeant.

"I thought they took that away from you," I said, tactfully.

His head jerked up. He made a harsh sound in his throat. "They couldn't find it to take away. It was unaccountably lost. Rose tell you I got busted?"

"Yes. She didn't say how."

"That ain't none of your business." He drank. "Who's this bimbo you want to find?"

"I don't know anything about him but this: he's a chunky little guy, about five eight or so. Likes sharp clothes. Wears a sky blue hat with a light-colored band. He likes shotguns, too. If you know him from that it'll be a miracle."

He stared down into his glass. "I was vice squad for fifteen years," he said. "I knew every gun in town. Intimately."

"How long you been busted?"

"Five months. Like I said, I knew 'em all. I knew everybody who came to town five minutes after they got off the plane. I knew Pete Mallory, too," he said, glancing up. "Even the ones who kept clean. I had to know. That was before I got busted. I was a conscientious bastard."

"Who's this one?"

"I think I know, but I could be wrong."

I grinned at him. "Sure. Fifteen years on the same beat. You could be wrong."

He grinned back sourly. "His name's Winkie Gilmer. A Southern boy, from Birmingham. Connected with Holtz in Buffalo once. Then a hired gun out of Cleveland for two years. Drifted in here seven months ago and caught on right away at Zavelli's luxury resort up the beach a few miles. Neptune Court. He don't do nothing much but sun himself and make out with the women. He disappears now and then for a week, ten days. Probably still freelances. He's twenty-four. He may have killed a dozen men."

"What's his talent?"

"Chiv."

"Thanks."

He poured himself another. "Don't mention it." He looked at me again, briefly. "You used to be up real high with Macy Barr. I thought you were out of that kind of work. I knew about you, but I never had the pleasure. Not that it's any pleasure."

"It gets into your blood, doesn't it?" I said.

"What?"

"The poison you make. Why keep the badge around? Think you might get to wear it again sometime?"

"Get out," he said dully.

"Okay." I stood up and walked around the bed. Then I stopped and reached for my wallet.

"I don't need it," he said. He looked around the room. "I got plenty."

"You gave me information I needed."

"I didn't do you no favor," he said. He laughed in an

ugly way. "This Gilmer is tough. He don't goof his jobs."

"He goofed one, or I wouldn't be talking to you now."

I got as far as the door this time. Then I swung around and his eyes were on me. They were the only bright spots in the dingy room.

"I hope you kill him," he said. "But only because it'll save some cop the trouble."

"You're all heart," I said.

He showed me his teeth. "I'm just a big, wonderful sucker," he said. "I could have made lieutenant. The only trouble was, I beat the hell out of my superior. Now why would I do that?"

"I wouldn't know," I said.

He looked down into the glass. "He was only making love to my wife," he said with a little sob. "Big hairy slob making love to my wife. No reason for me to smash his face for him, just over a little bit of tail that never was any good anyway." He began to laugh, rocking a little on the bed. "I could of been a lieutenant."

"Don't feel so bad," I told him. "Maybe somebody else will make you an angel." I shut the door as I went out. Rose sat with the puppy on the kitchen floor. I thanked her politely as I opened the door and started my descent down the back steps.

The sun was beginning to drop like a flat stone in deep water. I figured Gilmer could wait another hour. I wanted a shower and something to eat. It would give me an excuse to use the room I had bought for the mention of Macy's name. I wondered what else his name was buying these days. Not much, probably.

°

On my way to the hotel I stopped off long enough to buy a gun and some shoulder leather from a pawnshop owner who specialized in supplying iron to those who couldn't show a license. I knew all sorts of useless people like that. At the Coral Gardens I parked in the restricted zone under the eyes of a cop. He wasn't interested. I went on in and upstairs.

I was dressing after my shower when the phone rang.

"Yeah?"

"It's Macy, Pete. I thought you might be at the hotel. What's new?"

"I lucked out of a bomb try this morning, The boy who set the trap might be an ex-Cleveland hood named Winkie Gilmer. Apparently somebody's nervous about me looking around for the one survivor of the fire. Her name is Carla Kennedy. She'd be about thirty now."

"You've got a lead on her?"

"Yes. I won't know where she is until tomorrow night, though."

"How did you come up with this Gilmer?"

"Mostly luck. An ex-cop told me about him."

"What's Gilmer like?"

"I haven't met him yet. He's supposed to be tough. I've been warned off him. Strictly a hired gun. I'm interested in who hired him. He can't be very bright to wear a hat like that on a job. He might as well have had on a neon necktie."

"It sounds like a good break. Play it cool, Pete. You've been away a long time. Listen, stop by Stan's Restaurant and see if Diane is there."

"She hasn't showed up yet?"

"No. She sent the kid home with Taggart this afternoon. Aimee's cranky from those shots she got this morning. Tell Diane to pick up a car at the hotel and come on home. I don't like her wandering around after dark, anyway."

Chapter Fourteen

Stan's Restaurant was a low modern building with a curved roof and a front of thin orange bricks, fluted aluminum, chrome and glass blocks. His name blazed in the dusk in three-foot-high script letters. The restaurant was located on the flashy Rosamorada Strip eleven miles north of downtown and four blocks from Sunlan Park Race Track.

Inside, the restaurant was separated into dining room and bar by an angle of wall padded with leather-like material on the bar side. I looked into the dining room first. There was an overflow crowd, including a lot of small dark men in good suits and some who weren't so small, and beautiful women. The place was crawling with beautiful women, lean and fragile as expensive models. Yellow-jacketed waiters with placid expressions slipped between the full tables like good dancers, handling trays crisply.

I recognized a few faces: Suarez, king of the Spanish Town bug; Venetti, waterfront gambling; Scobey, whose bootlegging enterprise ran to tens of thousands of gallons a year. There were stills throughout the back country, and cars with heavy-duty springs in the back ends and trucks packed with large milk cans of the stuff were thick on crumbling, weed-lined roads every night. I stood there for a moment, picking out the faces, recognition coming from the nod of a head, the expansive lift of a hand.

Memories of a precarious time were sharp with the taste of danger light along the tongue. Annacone, call girls—and an uglier traffic in the merchandise of sex. There were strings tied to all of them, and to a hundred others scattered in half a dozen counties. Macy held all the strings, but not so securely any more.

The cuts came in by the week, by the month. Some of it was delivered, some had to be collected. There was always cheating. Books falsified. Revenues faked. It had been my job to see the rake-off was always right, to see that the boys who might be tempted to pocket too much never forgot how narrow the line was, how uncertain the balance of favor; to make sure they were always just a little bit uneasy, that they never stopped looking behind them when night came. It was dirty work. I did it competently. Still, there were always the bold, whose fingers were too sticky, whose appetites for the big piles of easy money were not diminished by the gentle prod of an unseen gun. Some of them were killed. Nothing pretty about it. The shotgun was usually the final judge of the sweet plunge into temptation. Sometimes they went into the bay, or a canal. I never knew when it would happen, or who would do it. I didn't want to know. I kept out of that. It was my only way of rebelling.

They would recognize me if I wanted them to see me. They would be secretly anxious behind big empty smiles. Maybe the strings were being slipped and cut now, the men under Macy growing plump on profits that brought less commission for Macy each month while the organization crumbled and he sat on his island playing with the child of a whore, a deep moan in his mind as he thought of a killer who waited for his chance. Maybe Stan Maxine was shifting the strings skillfully and discreetly to his own fingers. The cheating, the holding back always went on, even if the man who held the strings leaned on his employees ceaselessly, playing one against another, sending his own boys in unexpectedly to check and recheck operations. Macy had been that kind of leader once. Now the boys would be running wild, filling their pockets before the inevitable change of leadership and a new crackdown, an over-all tightening. So my reappearance would be an omen. Macy was trying to pull things back together. The last feeble blow from a declining giant. The word would go out, passed to silent men in obscure bars. Before the sun went down on another day, I'd be dead—unless I was incredibly lucky.

I pushed the thoughts away from my mind. I had enough to worry about. I went into the bar, which was about half full. On a small stage at the rear a Negro trio thumped out *Jumping the Boogie*. It was good barrelhouse stuff. I recognized one of the bartenders. He had once worked at the Coral Gardens, and he was good. Another gentle reminder that Stan was the fair-haired boy now. The flock came dutifully to his fancy watering hole.

"Hello, Paul," I said, leaning against the bar. He had hair like brushings from moths' wings, and his face was aging gracefully.

"Pete!" he said. "Pete, it's good to see you." A look of alarm killed the smile before it had a chance to widen. "You better get out of here, Pete."

"Why?"

He looked up and down the bar, leaned closer to me. "Stan's boys are turning this town upside down looking for you. It's a rush order. You're in bad trouble, son. Run for it."

"What is it? Why do they want me?"

"I don't know. The word was dropped. I'm telling you, Pete…"

"I saw Maxine once today. I don't get…"

"Play safe, Pete."

"Yeah. Okay. I'll clear out in a second. Have you seen a girl named Diane? She's wearing a green skirt and one of those pullover playshirts. Tall blonde. She may come around here once in a while."

"I know her. She was in about four this afternoon. I saw her with the boss."

"Stan?"

He nodded. "Yeah, Stan." He looked past me and the hollows in his cheeks deepened. "Oh, Lordy," he groaned. "Here comes trouble, Pete."

I turned around and put both elbows on the bar. They were on me already. One of them was tall and Irish-looking, with curly copper hair and a nose canted from too many beatings. The other one was shorter, wider, with about a quarter-inch of brown hair on his stone skull. His face was wider at the chin than through the forehead. He was wearing a purple necktie with a single streak of red in it.

"You Mallory?" Irish asked.

"That's right."

He was polite. "I'm O'Toole. This is Kostrakis. We've been looking for you."

"You found me," I said. "Shall we have a drink to celebrate?"

His lip arched slightly. The Greek didn't say a word. He just watched me.

"We don't have time. We're going to see Stan."

"What does he want?"

The Greek took one of my arms. He twisted it in such a way that his arm was inside my elbow, his hand on my wrist. He had a nerve under pressure in the wrist. With little effort on his part the arm could be broken.

"Let's walk on out," he said.

We went outside with the Greek at my side and O'Toole behind me. In the parking lot O'Toole moved up, edged the .38 from beneath my coat.

"I pulled the teeth," he said to the Greek. Kostrakis opened the door of a two-tone blue Chrysler and saw that I was seated comfortably before releasing the arm. He drove. O'Toole sat in back.

"Just take it easy," he advised. "Kostrakis, let's have some music." We had some music from the radio. O'Toole made small talk.

"Hear you used to work around these parts six or seven years ago. Ever know Vic Mount?" I never knew Vic Mount. "Cousin of mine. Used to pick up policy slips for Chiozza down around the Gresham Park district." It went like that. I kept my eyes on the streets we took, wondering where we were going. I was careful not to let the tiny growth of fear feed and enlarge in my tense mind.

We drove south on Rosamorada for a time, then turned right on Robinson Parkway, away from the bay. Ten minutes later we were at Lake Alena and we took a left at Jacaranda, the street on which Stan lived. In another minute we cut through an alley and pulled into a two-car garage. I was hustled through the darkened yard into Maxine's kitchen. The boys weren't trying so hard to be gentle now.

Stan was in the living room. When I was shown in he glanced at me, his face unnaturally composed. He got up and pulled the blinds down over the front windows. He turned to me, his mouth set in anguished lines. "Nice of you to come."

"It wasn't my choice."

"Where is she?"

"Where is who?"

"You know who. You know who I'm talkin' about. Gerry. Where's Gerry? What did you do with her, you bastard?" His breath spurted frantically from his lungs, betraying his unhealthiness.

"Hold on, Maxine. I don't know—"

He stepped closer to me. Kostrakis turned at my side, bringing his fist up. "Let me," Maxine whispered, his eyes full of tearful rage. His tongue pried his lips apart. Sweat glistened in the holes of his cheeks. His fist doubled. I moved my shoulders forward, balancing on the pads of my feet. Stan hesitated. "Hold him."

Fingers closed around my arms, yanked them back and away from my sides. Maxine grunted and drove his fist into my gut. One of my legs bounced up. I couldn't double over to ease the pain. I kicked out at him but there was no strength in the kick. It missed.

"Where did you take Gerry? Where is she? Damn you, Mallory, where's my girl?"

I couldn't say anything. I strained for breath, my eyes weeping from the effort. I knew my face must be darkening.

When I could speak I told him, "I don't know where she is. I care less. You crazy or something, Maxine?"

"You want her, don't you?" he said. "I could tell today. Saw you looking at her. Where did you go with her?"

"You're nuts. I don't touch it unless it's been aged at least twenty years."

He moaned and hit me again. This time I managed to shy to one side so his blow grazed my ribs first. I writhed helplessly, clamped between the two big men.

"You scum," I said, my teeth tightly together. "What makes you think she didn't run off? What makes you think she'd want to hang around you long? You got sex appeal or something?"

His eyes pressed shut. He swayed a little. "Get him out of here," he whimpered. "Get him out of here before I kill him! Find out if he's lying."

They jerked me around and dragged me through the dining room and kitchen. My arms were numb from the grip of their fingers, swift needles of pain breaking in my palms and fingers. This time I went into the back seat of the Chrysler, face down on the floor. My head was held fast with a double length of rope fastened to a pair of hooks embedded in the floor, and passed across the back of my neck. It was hard for me to find a place for my legs. I finally had to bend them under me and lie cramped in the small space, my face scraping against the rough hairy matting at every bounce. There were a lot of bounces, because Kostrakis was an arrogant driver with a heavy right foot. Before long I was feeling calm, cold fury. They had my gun. But if I had just one, tiny chance I would try to get them with my hands.

The ride was endless. Once there was the jostle of railroad tracks, then the Klaxon of a boat. The blare of horns came less frequently, and there were fewer traffic lights. I became resigned to spending the rest of my life tied to that swaying floor. The fury lessened. I wanted a drink of water. My throat was rougher than the floor covering. I wanted to stretch out my legs. I could feel the throaty drum of the motor as speed increased. Maybe we would be there soon—wherever we were going. Then they would let me up. I thought no further than the mercy of being released from the floor of that car.

The Chrysler slowed down, lurched as tires bumped off the pavement. Gravel crackled and splattered under the wheels as the front end nosed downward. A few seconds of this and we stopped. Doors opened. Cool air feathered my hair. Something tugged at the ropes across my neck and they parted. I shifted position cautiously, rubbing at the stiff, fiery muscles.

"Get out," the Greek said.

I put an arm over the front seat, dragged my legs forward, stepped out of the car. I had to lean against the door to stand. There was enough light to see that we were on the edge of swampland. I smelled the marshy water. Close to the Chrysler was the steel framework of a trestle for a huge steam shovel or crane.

They went to work without speaking. A hand closed on my shirt and I was jerked forward. Another hand chopped down swiftly, the palm edge hitting with blunt shock at the base of my neck, near the ridge of collarbone. I felt the blow to my fingertips, bit off a groan and dropped to my knees in the gravel.

Somewhere nearby, tires streaked the pavement as a car slowed suddenly, pitched off the highway. Headlights fanned toward us as the car skidded down the embankment, showering gravel. I looked up and saw the face of Kostrakis pinched with surprise in the sudden light. His hand made a move toward his coat, stopped, dropped to his side.

I looked around and saw Taggart and Reavis, the gatekeeper, getting out of the car. I stood up wearily.

"You guys want something?" O'Toole said angrily. Reavis went up to him and hit him with a long slashing fist. O'Toole arched backwards, fingers curling, and sprawled downhill, rolling loosely to the edge of weedy dark water. Kostrakis looked over his shoulder at him and kept his mouth shut.

"What are you boys doing here?" I said, holding my bruised shoulder.

Taggart tipped his massive head toward the car. Rudy was sitting behind the wheel and there was a blonde in the back seat.

"Diane saw you walk into trouble at Maxine's," he said. "She called us. We figured you'd show up here sooner or later. Maxine's boys favor this place for staying in shape. They stay in shape by beating hell out of guys like you. Right, Greek?"

Kostrakis said nothing.

"Unload your iron," Reavis said. His coat was open and he had a hand near the gun on his belt.

Kostrakis slipped a hand inside his coat, unholstered the gun with great care.

"On the ground," Reavis said. The revolver arced to the gravel.

"Pick it up," Taggart said.

Kostrakis swallowed. He tried to stoop and pick the

gun up while looking at Taggart. His hand couldn't find it. He had to look. When he did Taggart stepped forward and smashed a knee into his face. The Greek slumped back against the door of the car, sitting down. His face was bloody from forehead to chin. As he breathed, bubbles formed at his mashed nostrils. He leaned forward, put his hands in the gravel and crawled like a chubby, awkward baby toward the gun.

Taggart grinned and kicked the revolver away. It skidded down the slope and plopped into the water. Taggart kicked Kostrakis in the face. The Greek passed out. Taggart prodded him with a foot and he rolled gently after the gun, his bleeding face picking up dirt and loose gravel. Taggart looked after him indifferently.

"If you're all rescued," he said to me, "let's go."

I took my gun from the glove compartment of the Chrysler, followed Reavis and Taggart to their car. I got into the back seat with Diane. Rudy turned around cautiously and we edged up the incline to the highway.

"Thanks for spotting me," I said to Diane. "I would have picked up a good pounding down there."

"Why did Stan do that?" she said.

"You were with him all afternoon. You ought to know."

"Sorry, I don't," she said unemotionally.

"He thinks I ran off with his woman."

"I suppose you didn't."

"In a way. But I didn't touch her. He's crazy jealous. What were you two doing today?"

"I—there was someplace I wanted to go. We went together."

"Like where?"

"Why should I tell you?"

"Like where?"

"Lay off the goddam questions," Taggart said.

"Shut your face," I told him. "I wasn't talking to you."

I saw his shoulders heave, but he didn't turn around.

"Easy," Rudy murmured. "Somewhere you want to go?"

"Stan's Restaurant," I said. "I'll pick up the car there. You take Diane home. Macy's been worried about the company she keeps."

She squirmed in the seat with her arms folded across her breasts, stared out the window. A blank sullen silence closed around all of us.

Chapter Fifteen

The desk clerk at the Coral Gardens Hotel told me Owen Barr had left the hotel an hour ago. I walked through the sedate lobby to the basement steps and went downstairs, opened the door of Owen's little retreat. I couldn't find a light switch anywhere. Grayish light from the windows was pinned to the tarpaulin on one wall and a long bar of it slanted across the dirty floor and crept up one of the old sofas, affectionately grasped a girl's small bare foot.

I shut my eyes tightly and waited for a few seconds. When I opened my eyes again I could see more clearly. Gerry was lying on the sofa on her back, sound asleep. She was mother-naked, but not like mother ever was. Her nudity irritated me somehow. I had nearly got my head knocked off while she slept comfortably down here.

I walked over to the sofa and smacked her with the flat of my hand on her bare thigh. She jerked awake and moved her legs. She put one hand on the assaulted leg.

"Hey! Wha—" She struggled to focus her sleepy eyes on me. "Who are you?"

"Mallory."

"Oh." She winced. "What did you do that for?"

"Get up and get dressed," I said. "People are looking for you."

She slid her knees beneath her, kneeled on the sofa,

facing me, raised her head. "That really stings," she complained. She yawned huskily, touching her hair with her fingers, then raised her arms full-length. Her breasts swelled high.

I noticed her clothing on the table with Owen's tubes of color. I turned around and picked up the red pants, underclothes, brief blouse. I tossed the clothing at her. "Put these on."

"What for?"

"You're going back to Stan."

She slid her legs over the edge of the sofa, sat up. "I don't think I want to go back," she said stubbornly.

"You're going back," I promised her, "if I have to carry you out of here dressed the way you aren't."

She laughed incredulously. "You wouldn't—"

I stepped toward her quickly, caught one of her wrists, brought her stiffly to her feet. She hesitated, then leaned against me, teasing me with a motion of her hips. Her eyelids drooped. "We don't have to go back right now. We could—"

I wasn't enchanted. She was a brat. But even feeling that way I had to get the weight of the lusty body away from me. I shoved her roughly, letting go the wrist.

"What's the matter?" she said. "Don't you like women?"

"You're not a woman. You're a shallow-brained little girl rattling around in a woman's body. Get dressed, damn you."

The scornful edge of my voice stung worse than the slap I had given her. She shifted her weight uncertainly from one bare foot to the other, then sniffed, then sat down on the sofa, still looking at me. She picked up her brassiere, fitted it to her breasts, fastened it. She stood up, holding her panties. Without turning away she stepped into them, pulled them up slowly over her legs, her full thighs. She spread her legs slightly, patted the tight sheer panties into place. She never took her eyes off me. I walked away from her in irritation and waited until she was finished dressing.

When she had everything in place, we went through the dimly lighted basement and out the back way. I held firmly to her wrist until she was safe in the front seat of the Buick.

"Was Stan worried about me?" she said in a tiny voice.

"Oh, *boy*," I said. It was all the talking we did until we reached Stan's house. Once there she got out of the car reluctantly, then straightened her shoulders resolutely and walked firmly up to the front door and inside. I followed her.

Maxine was pouring a drink and when he saw Gerry the neck of the bottle chattered against the glass, whisky spilling.

"Gerry!"

"Hello, Stan," she said calmly.

A couple of the boys watching TV in one corner looked up briefly, then returned their attentions to the set. I hadn't seen them before.

Maxine put both hands around the glass. He looked past Gerry at me. "Well, where you been?" he said, still shaken. He wasn't quite able to work himself into a rage. "Well, where's *she* been?" he demanded of me. I didn't say anything. I just looked at him.

He rubbed his forehead. His eyes were on Gerry. "I

looked for you," he said. "You weren't anywhere around." His fists clenched. He glanced at me again. "We'll talk about it later," he said grimly to Gerry.

"Okay," Gerry said. She swallowed once, then turned precisely and walked toward the kitchen. "I'm going to get something to eat," she said.

Stan looked at her, his lips tight. "All right. There's ham sandwiches in the icebox. I'll be along in a second."

When she had pushed through the door Maxine looked at me. He put the overflowing glass down and walked toward me. He took a long breath, held it, released it little by little.

"Well, where did you find her?"

"She can tell you if she wants to. I won't."

He glanced toward his boys. "You—" the word whistled through the crack between his lips. "You knew where she was all the time."

"Maybe."

"What happened to Kostrakis and O'Toole?"

"They had an accident."

There was disgust on his face. "Maybe one of these days I'll get somebody I can depend on." He whipped another look at the Home Guard. They dropped their eyes guiltily to the television screen.

Stan lowered his voice. "I want to know where Gerry was. Did she go to see somebody? I got to know if she's been playing around."

The dining-room door was pushed open. "I went to the library," Gerry said. She had a sandwich and a glass of milk.

"All afternoon?"

Gerry nodded.

"What were you doing?" Maxine said with a crazy smile.

"Reading a book."

Maxine turned to me. He pointed to Gerry, speechless.

"You heard what she said," I told him.

Stan chuckled, then went into a spasm of violent laughter that left him clutching his stomach, his face the color of greasy cream. He had to sit down. Gerry looked concerned.

"Stan? Are you—"

"Nah, I'm all right," he said, the words riding on an indrawn breath. "What are you hanging around for?" he snapped at me.

"I did you a favor. Now you do me one."

His lower lip crawled away from his teeth. "Like what?"

"Diane was with you today, wasn't she?"

"For a little while this afternoon."

"You know her pretty well."

"Some. She used to work for me."

"Which doesn't tell me anything."

He showed me his palms. "So what do you want? We're kind of good friends. She comes in once in a while."

"You know anything about her?"

"Like?"

"Where she came from."

"Nah, I don't—I never asked. Why would I?"

"She ever do anything crazy around you?"

"Crazy?" He had to think about it. "Nah, nothing crazy. She was—different. But she never did anything crazy."

"One thing more. You know Winkie Gilmer?"

He was bored. He shook his head. "I never heard the

name." I was watching the boys at the TV set, too. Nobody twitched.

Gerry sat down beside Stan on the sofa, nuzzled him. He stiffened, then let himself be petted. He took one of her hands, held it with beautiful tenderness. I tried to keep from sneering as I walked out of the house and shut the door behind me with a light click.

The Neptune Court occupied two blocks of beach land on a narrow peninsula known as Fontaine Beach. It was a mushrooming resort center. Ornate motels and hotels done in bold long lines sprawled along the strip of highway in a growing chain. Every day bulldozers scraped at the raw land while sun-reddened men with fat stacks of blueprints watched and planned. The street crumbled slowly under the impact of the ready-mix trucks.

The motor court was a two-story Y-shaped building a block long, the two prongs of the Y set at an angle against the shoreline, which had been filled in here and there and otherwise contrived so that from every room in the court a bit of blue water could be seen. There was a large swimming pool in the juncture of the Y, then a hedge of Australian pine and beyond that a string of cabanas on the beach. Down one side of the court was a deep wide gash that served as a harbor for visiting yachts and small craft.

Zavelli's restaurant and night club was set apart from the main building, connected to it by an arcade with small shops. There was dancing on the secluded roof of the club and pale tuneless music glittered in the air.

They told me inside I could find Zavelli on the roof.

I went up the outside stairway. There was iron grill-work around the parapet and some kind of hedge. The dance floor and the ring of tables were on different levels. A man in a dinner jacket stopped me under the entrance arch.

"You don't go in without a tie."

"Zavelli in there?"

"Maybe."

"You go and tell him Pete Mallory wants him."

He looked me over with a calm practiced eye. "What was the name?"

I told him again.

"It don't mean nothing to me."

"It rhymes with Macy Barr."

His monotonous stare broke up. "Wait here," he said. He went inside. I watched a tired tango on the dance floor below. He came back and took me to a table in one corner of the shelf above the dance floor. Zavelli sat there in a built-up chair. He had a normal-sized head, but his body was stunted, the arms grotesquely short, shoulders narrow and sloping.

"Sit down," he said in a yawning voice. There was an intermission below and a shuffle of feet past his isolated table, a crackle of female laughter. He watched the dancers go by with no change of expression. "How's Macy these days?"

"You don't know?"

"I've heard things." He looked at me with a hint of expectancy. "What can I do you for?"

"You got a boy named Winkie Gilmer?"

"Yes."

"What's he do?"

"I use him downstairs. Keeps things orderly."

"Kind of a waste of his talents, isn't it?"

"I didn't know he had any."

"You know as well as I do that he's a hired gun and anything he does around here is a blind. Don't stall me, Zavelli. I want him. Right now. He's up to his ears with me. You get him or you close down."

His thin chest quaked. "He ain't been around in a couple of days."

"Where is he?"

"I don't know."

"He hire out much?"

"I—don't know. That's his business."

"Who sent him here?"

He tipped a glass to his lips, holding it with both miniature hands. "Groaner. From Cleveland."

"To do whose work?"

"I don't know. I don't ask."

"Any more in town like him?"

He turned the sorrowful eyes on me. "Couldn't tell you, Mallory. I stick close to my place. I don't hear everything that goes on."

"All right. Forget it. I want to see Gilmer's room."

Zavelli raised one of his short arms high. Near the entrance, the man in the dinner jacket was leaning against one of the posts of the ivy-roofed arch. He came to the table.

"Take him to Gilmer's room," Zavelli said. The man glanced at me curiously. We went downstairs and walked through the arcade and entered the lobby of the motel. He took a key from the desk and we went to Gilmer's room. He stood by the door while I looked around.

There was a single bed, night stand, three chairs, desk, dresser, all made of bleached wood. There was no suitcase in the closet. A beach robe and a wrinkled sport shirt were on hangers, and a pair of canvas shoes was stacked in a corner like nervous feet. A Polaroid camera with flash attachment in a leather carrying case hung from a hook on the closet door.

In one of the desk drawers I found a folder of pictures. All of them had been taken with the Polaroid. There were all kinds of women in the pictures, most of them young, some trying hard to seem young, women in beds, bathtubs, automobiles. Some wore an occasional article of clothing, some were happily getting rid of it. Most wore nothing. Winkie was a souvenir hunter.

I turned the wastebasket upside down but it was empty. So were the dresser drawers. A big Zenith portable radio and his little camera seemed to be Winkie's chief amusements. I checked the medicine cabinet in the bathroom and found only suntan oil, dull razor blades.

"You know Gilmer?" I said to the man in the dinner jacket. He nodded mechanically, his jaw grinding chewing gum.

"What kind of car's he drive?"

"Buick Century. New."

"He got any girlfriends around this place?"

The man laughed drily. "Mister, Winkie's had 'em all."

I grinned a little. I took out the .38 automatic and let him get a good look at it. He couldn't take his eyes away. He wasn't that kind of tough guy—yet.

I jacked a shell out of the chamber and the slide

slammed forward. I bounced the cartridge in my hand, tossed it at him. He caught it and held it with two fingers.

"You see Winkie around here any time soon," I said, "give him that." I put the .38 away and walked past him into the hall.

"And tell him I've got six more just like it I'm going to stick square in his gut the first time I see him."

Chapter Sixteen

It was eleven o'clock when I drove down the causeway to the island and was let through the gate by a hobbling Rudy. The house was quiet.

Macy Barr wasn't in his study. The door was open slightly and a lamp on the desk was lighted. I pushed the door out of the way and went inside, intending to wait for him there.

In one corner, near the desk, there was a small safe. The door hadn't been shut tightly. Macy probably kept money for household expenses in the safe. A tightening excitement concentrated my attention on that safe. It would be a good place for keeping certain papers close at hand. Not his own papers, but a file of reports and notes about, and signed by, other men over whom it was necessary to exercise control.

I walked closer to the flimsy little safe, feeling almost giddy with anticipation. If I could find it, I thought. If I could find the letter—

The safe door opened readily, squeaking slightly. I ignored the packages of small bills, leafed through the contents of a clasp envelope, glancing at the first paragraphs of letters that were meaningless to me, looking for the address of a New York sanitarium on the fronts of the old envelopes stuck here and there in the collection of papers. I was too intent on my search to hear Macy when he came in.

"Pete. *Pete!*"

I shoved the bulky envelope back into the safe and jerked around. Macy watched me with a furious expression that slowly changed to one of mere tiredness.

"You know," he said, "I've got a gun in this pocket. In the old days, or just a couple of years ago, I'd have shot you dead without even asking you what you thought you were doing."

I stood up, unable to say anything, my mouth tight with apprehension. He never took his eyes off me. He pulled the .45 out of the pocket of his robe an inch at a time. He glanced down at it in exasperation, let it drop back.

"So you want the letter," Macy said. "What were you going to do with it, Pete? Rip it up and burn it and go your way?"

I didn't speak. "You answer me!" he shouted, losing control for a moment.

"I don't know," I said thickly.

Macy walked to his desk, his face rigid with a sort of pain. "Sit down, Pete, and listen to me. If you walk away now so help me I'll kill you."

He took a key from a holder he carried and unlocked a drawer of the desk. He took out a cardboard box and untied a string around it with clumsy shaking fingers. He sorted through the stuff inside as if he couldn't quite remember what was there. Then he stopped, shook a soiled folded envelope free, looked it over, put it on the edge of his desk.

"Look at it," he said gruffly.

I did. It was the one. I opened the envelope to make sure.

Macy grunted harshly, leaned out of the chair and

grasped the wastebasket beside the desk. It banged against the desk as he upended it. The contents of the wastebasket were scattered on the floor. He heaved it to the desk, stood up, picked up a cigarette lighter. He held the letter with one hand and set fire to it. When it was burning good he dropped it into the wastebasket and sat down again. The burning left a sour brown smell in the room.

"There it is, Pete," he said. "You can go now, if that's all that was keeping you here. I never would have used it. I never would have sent it to your girlfriend. It was a bluff. Just bluff. That's all I am now, bluff."

He stood up and turned around and kicked the chair he had been sitting in. It flipped over and banged into the wall nearby. "Go on, get out of here. Go back to your girl, Pete. Hang on to her. Hang on to her as if you never had anything in your life before. Because you never did, till you had her."

"If I leave," I said, "somebody's going to kill you. He may do it anyway."

His head hung for a moment. "I know it," he said as though he had just at that moment begun to realize it.

"You're a sad sight, Macy," I said. I didn't know why I was going to say the things that had been collecting in my mind. I knew it wouldn't help now, but this man had been a second father to me once, in his own way. "Every two-bit racketeer in this area has his hand in your back pocket. The wolves are circling, and Maxine's leading the pack. What the hell you been doing?" He just looked sullen and a little bit pitiful.

"Who's supposed to be taking care of things in town for you?" I said, trying to punch the right key to make him react.

"Reavis," he said. "Reavis handles most of the work you used to do. Taggart does most of the traveling."

"What kind of job is Reavis doing?"

"Lousy."

"Not that I care, but can him and get a new bunch. The pilings are rotten, Macy, and the whole works is coming down around your ears. I was in town one day, and I can see it."

"Let up on me! I know it. I know."

"But you don't give a damn."

He tried to fling an answer at me. Nothing came. He jammed his hands into his pockets.

"What's got into you?" I said. "The kid? Aimee? Did that start it? Or were you already coming unstuck when she came along? Now a crackbrain killer has thrown a scare into you. You used to have steel walls around you, but when you weren't looking somebody stole them, and all that's left is cardboard. A handful of men and a book-keeper are all you got left. No wonder you're shaking."

"Pete! Will you leave it alone, Pete? I did you a favor, what do you want? Will you leave it alone, Pete!" I didn't know whether or not he meant it, but he had pulled the automatic from his pocket and was pointing it at me.

"Put it down," I said, wondering how touchy the trigger might be. A coldness spread from the roof of my mouth to my chest.

He looked down at the gun, puzzled. He put his other hand over his chin, and the barrel of the .45 dipped slowly, as if his wrist muscles were stretching.

"I think we need a drink," he said then.

"Let's have a drink," I agreed breathlessly.

There was a bar in the living room, with a small refrigerator. We went there. He mixed the drinks and made them strong. We sat in two stylish chairs, facing each other uncertainly. Macy lifted his glass to me.

"You're right, Pete," he said. "I don't know when it started. Maybe as far back as six years ago. It hasn't been anything sudden. A little ground lost here and there, not recovered. Some cheating overlooked because it wasn't quite so important at the time. Things got loose. I didn't stay around town enough. It was better down here. Last year I moved. I stay here all the time now. With Aimee.

"I wasn't completely unaware of what was happening, Pete. I thought I could step back in any time I wanted. Give the orders. Clean things up. Then one day it was too late. It didn't even seem to matter much. I knew then how old I was getting. I tried just to hold things as they were. Tell myself it really wasn't as bad as it looked, that nobody realized. But everybody knew. My own boys knew first. A few of them left. They went over to Maxine. The others got sloppy. Now Maxine's getting ready to make his bid. It's not worth fighting back."

"What are you going to do when the showdown finally comes?"

"There won't be any showdown," he said, but his eyes were evasive. He had something in mind but wasn't ready to talk about it. "Tell me what happened today, Pete. Everything."

I told him. "Both Gilmer and Carla Kennedy are important," I finished. "When I find either of them I may know who's been sending you fan mail."

"Rudy doesn't sleep any more," Macy said reflectively. "I look at Rudy and say that it doesn't bother me like that, but it does." He swirled ice in his glass, drained the last of the whisky. "I ought to tell you to go home, Pete," he said without shame, "but I'm afraid to. I want you around."

He frowned, hearing what I had been hearing. It was a woman's hard ugly scream mixed with a man's thick-voiced, shouted curses. Macy sat up straight in his chair. "What the hell is that? They'll wake Aimee." He ran heavily from the living room and I followed, wincing at the searing, uncontrolled hate underscoring the shouts.

In the wing of the house where my room was, I saw Owen Barr wrestling, bearlike, with a woman. It was Diane. She hit him in the face, the fingers of her hand slightly curled and stiff. He was having a hard time with her. He bounced her off a wall and she tried to kick him between the legs. He lowered one shoulder, dug it into her stomach, brought it up hard to smash across one breast.

Diane spat at him. She spat until her mouth was dry, and clawed at the top of his head. Hair hung down on her face. She tried to thumb his eyes, but he kept his face down. One of her feet kicked through a pane of the French doors and blood gleamed at her ankle. The raw animal fury in her face slowed my step for an instant. There was a dribbling of saliva from her mouth. She screamed hoarsely, over and over. Owen muttered guttural curses.

His hands closed over the blouse she wore and there was a sharp ripping noise. Diane was suddenly still. Owen grabbed her by the neck and threw her into his room, catching her wrist as she stumbled. Diane searched for the tear, found it under one arm. A bit of her skin showed through the frayed material at her armpit. She tried to kick Owen but he kept out of her way. She wasn't screaming any more, but breathed with a slight snarl, like a cornered lioness. There was a chilling blank look in her eyes, as if she saw nothing.

Macy went into the bedroom. I stood in the doorway.

"Look at it!" Owen screamed. "Look at it! You ruined it! Bitch. Bitch!" He lunged forward and his small fat palm flew upward in a big arc to crack across her face with a nasty meaty sound. It snapped her head back and knocked her halfway around. She would have fallen if Owen hadn't held her wrist. There was blood on his lower lip where he had bitten it in rage.

"She slashed my painting," Owen sobbed indignantly, jerking at the moaning Diane. "She—"

I heard someone behind me but had no chance to move before a big hand shoved me out of the doorway. I pitched inside and Taggart shouldered past me. "He hit her!" Taggart groaned. He reached for Owen and threw him against the wall. Diane slumped to the floor. Taggart put his economy-sized hands around Owen's throat. Tendons stretched like cables as the fingers squeezed. I saw helpless fear widen Owen's eyes as his mouth spread open.

I wedged myself between Owen and Taggart, shoved his powerful arms up and apart, then pushed my neck and shoulders hard into his stomach, bracing myself with a foot against the wall. I sensed the hands coming loose from Owen's throat and threw myself against Taggart. We hit the floor together. I was on top. He pushed me away, got up slowly, one knee down. I belted him in the gut. It stopped him for maybe a couple of seconds. Then he pulled the other leg up and started for Owen, who gibbered with fright at the approach of the big man.

"He hit her," Taggart said. "I'll kill him!" He got one of the hands around Owen's throat again. He used the other to hold me off.

"Stop it," Macy said. "Diane, tell him to stop it!"

"Tag," Diane said weakly. It was a small sound but he heard it. He eased his hand away and Owen slid to the floor. He put his head down and crawled away from us into the hall.

Taggart looked at me for a few charged seconds, then made a gesture that indicated I was of no consequence. He glanced at Diane. I thought he was going to go to her but he just watched her get off the floor.

"What is this?" Macy said. "What the hell happened here?" He looked from Owen to Diane.

Owen leaned against the doorframe, sobbing for breath. "I caught her coming...out of my room," he said. He pointed to one of the many oil paintings on the wall. "She...slashed it. The dirty goddam bitch slashed my... painting." He started to cry.

We looked at the picture he was talking about. It was a seascape. Somebody had taken a knife or razor blade to it. The canvas was in tatters.

"You come in here and do that?" Macy said threateningly.

Diane turned her head to look at the picture. Her face was beginning to get that smooth motionless look. Owen's slap had snapped her loose from something that had been building up within her. "I came in here. I just wanted to look at them. I wasn't going to hurt anything."

"She cut it!" Owen blubbered sickeningly, hanging on to the doorframe.

I saw Charley Rinke standing behind him in the hall, watching with an oddly fascinated expression.

"I didn't touch your picture," Diane said, with a trace of contempt. "I don't have anything to cut with." Her voice was becoming remote. She looked at the blood on her ankle.

"You gonna believe her? I caught her coming out! She did it! Shediditshediditshe—"

Macy walked up to his brother and hit him across the face with the back of his hand. Owen shut up. There was a look of bewilderment in his eyes. He put out a hand, gropingly.

"Macy…"

"Shut up, you fool," Macy said in a deadly calm voice.

Owen's face changed gradually, stiffening into hate that was deep and aching. He straightened up and his breathing slowed. He looked coldly at Macy. It was a look that had taken him all his life to achieve, and in a way it was a frightening thing. He saved some of it for Diane. She looked back without flinching. Owen turned and walked down the hall, his body stiff, his legs wobbling slightly. He looked straight ahead. In a few seconds the front door slammed, but not loudly.

Macy's gaze shifted to the ruined painting, and his mouth softened. "Goddam fool," he muttered almost tenderly. "All right," he said, looking about him. "What the hell are you all standing around for? Clear out. You, Taggart, get out of here. Rinke, get back to the books."

They drifted away slowly, and the knotted tension slackened. Diane didn't move until the others had gone.

"You get, too," Macy said to her. "Clean yourself up.

You look like you been raped in a telephone booth."

Diane didn't look at either of us. She went out, taking care not to step too hard on the ankle that had been hurt. The cut didn't look deep. I could see through the tear in her blouse at the armpit. She held that arm close to her side.

Macy looked at the torn painting again. "Now what the hell got into that crazy dame?" he said.

"You think she cut it?" I asked him.

"Sure I think she cut it." He made a fist and put his other hand over it. "Oh, well. They ain't worth nothing anyway."

"Owen seemed pretty upset."

"My little brother," Macy said scornfully. "Aw, he'll get over it. I guess I'd better go upstairs and see if the ruckus woke Aimee up. She ain't feeling so good. Come on."

Chapter Seventeen

Aimee was lying awake in bed when we came in. She blinked at the sudden light. There were drying tears on her cheeks. The bed sheets were twisted.

"Was Diane yelling?" she said, and began to cry again. Macy picked her up and held her gently.

"It wasn't anything," he said. "Diane's all right. She'll come upstairs and go to bed with you pretty soon."

"I can't sleep," Aimee moaned.

"Your stomach still upset?"

Aimee nodded. She chewed on the knuckles of one fist.

Macy looked at me. "Get her some water, will you, Pete? There's some capsules in there, too. Bring one."

I went into the bathroom. I could hear him talking to her, soothingly, in a voice I had rarely heard him use. I ran water into a glass and picked up one of the capsules.

Macy put it between Aimee's stiff lips, gave her some water. She swallowed dutifully. "That'll help," Macy said encouragingly. "Your tummy will feel better."

"Are we going to go boat riding tomorrow?" Aimee whimpered.

"Well…I don't think so, baby. Daddy's still busy. I'll tell you what. One day soon we're going to go on a long boat ride. For months and months. Would you like that?"

I hoped the boat ride he had in mind wouldn't be across the Styx.

She nodded enthusiastically. "Where we goin', Daddy?"

"I'm not sure yet. But we're going. I promise you that. We'll go places we've never been to, and we'll have a good time together."

"Can Diane go, too?"

"Sure," Macy said, after a quick pause. "Diane can go, too."

He put Aimee back into bed and tucked the sheet around her. He took a book from the bedside table and began to read to her. He had to hold the book fairly close to his face so he could see the print. I hung around feeling useless until Diane came in. She had washed her face and combed her hair, but the blouse was still torn. There was a puffiness about her eyes. She took a clean blouse from her dresser and went into the bathroom to change.

Aimee went to sleep in the midst of a sentence and Macy put up the book with some reluctance; he was enjoying the story.

We went downstairs. "Let's go to the garage," he said without hesitation. "Something you ought to see."

I followed him outside to the garage. At the rear of the building he pointed to a large wooden box, about four feet long, filled with old tires and odds and ends of junk.

"Pull it this way," he said. I put my hands on the box. It moved with astonishing ease, soundlessly. The frame of the box was mounted on rollers. Under it was a flight of steps. Two small square lights studding the concrete sides of the staircase provided illumination.

We descended. I went first. Macy reached up and pulled the box back over the entrance. It bumped snugly against the back wall of the garage. I stooped to go through a doorway at the base of the steps, found myself in a good-sized room with a low ceiling. It was air conditioned. The walls were lined with some kind of acoustical material, tinted pastel yellow. There were fluorescent lights screwed to the ceiling. Charley Rinke worked at a long table, his shirt sleeves rolled up. He was surrounded by stacks of account books, papers held together with rubber bands, boxes, a filing cabinet drawer. He looked haggard, glanced up quickly when we came in, then went back to work with an adding machine. Paper littered the floor. There was a full ashtray beside Rinke's elbow, and a pitcher of water.

"This is what you might call the nerve center, Pete," Macy said quietly. "I hate all this bookwork, but it's necessary." He walked quickly to a large safe with a formidable gray steel door. The safe was embedded in concrete at the back wall of the room. He swung the door open, gestured toward the safe.

"Better to have all this here than in town," Macy explained. "Any trouble at the gates and I can seal this room up with a couple tons of broken concrete. Take a steam shovel to find anything, even if somebody wanted to go to the trouble of ferrying one out here."

Rinke made a final calculation on the adding machine, yawned, threw down his pencil and got up to join us.

There was a lot of cash in the safe. Enough to make me wonder what it would be like to own that much, at one time, to be able to pick it up in neat packages, stack it, look at it.

"How much?" I said.

"I'm not sure," Macy said. "It would take two large suitcases to hold all of it, and most of the bills are hundreds. A few fifties, some twenties. Altogether, about three quarters of a million dollars. I've got more, of course. Stashed in three banks. The money I pay tax on." He shut the safe, pushing with both hands against the door.

"He's giving it all up," Rinke said, in a nervously high voice. He cleared his throat. "He's giving all of it to Maxine. All of it."

"That's right," Macy said, not looking at Rinke.

Rinke gave me a guarded look, wondering what I thought about it. His lips were thin with anger.

"Maxine's coming here tomorrow night," Barr said lightly. "I'm telling him then." He looked around the room. "I don't want it no more. None of it. I'm taking what money I can and I'm leaving the country."

"Macy—" Rinke said tenaciously, as if he were preparing to reopen an argument that had flourished for days.

"I don't want to hear no more," Macy said. "You got your work to do. Just do it and don't bother me. Don't give me any pep talks. Don't try to talk me into something I don't want to do. I just want out. That's all."

Rinke took a pack of cigarettes from his shirt pocket. He lit one, steadying his hand. "Okay, Macy," he said. "Okay, I won't try to say anything to you." He walked to the table, then turned suddenly, pointing with the cigarette, words tumbling.

"But he's coming here. He's coming here tomorrow night, and he's walking right into our hands. Maybe two or three men, that's all he'll bring with him. Can't you see it? It'd be so easy then to get rid of him—"

"Shut up!" Macy rasped. Then, more quietly, "Shut up, Charley. Don't try to put ideas in my head I don't

want to hear." He snorted. "Charley, sometimes I think
you want to run this outfit."

Rinke turned away, tapped a couple of keys on the
adding machine. "Okay," he said, resignedly. "Forget it."
I sensed again a silent appeal from him, from the staring
magnified eyes. When I didn't respond he sat down and
went back to work, doggedly, flipping the stiff pages of a
ledger with competent fingers, making notations with his
pencil. I wondered if he still nourished the rebellious
thoughts far back in his mind, where they wouldn't get in
the way of the precise click of integers.

Chapter Eighteen

Later that night I awakened sitting straight up in bed, muscles tense. For a few seconds I had no idea where I was. I felt a sense of dread, as if I were being watched from the sable darkness around me. I breathed deeply, ridding my throat of deep panic. I stood up and walked to the windows, looked out. It was after one o'clock.

I dressed, putting on the shoulder holster over my shirt, and went into the hall. The door to Owen's room was open, but he wasn't inside. I went upstairs. There were no lights on, but moonlight thinned the darkness. At Macy's room I tapped softly on the door. There was no answer. I listened closely, heard him breathing in sleep.

At the end of the hall a door was open and I saw Mrs. Rinke inside, standing in front of a window, looking toward the sea. She had been in bed. The other bed hadn't been touched. Apparently Rinke was still working.

As I turned to walk away my shoe bumped the doorframe. It was a small noise, but Evelyn Rinke turned, a hand at her throat, a flat cry on her lips.

I stepped inside the bedroom so she could identify me. She was wearing the same nightgown she had had on the night before.

"Pete?"

"Yes."

"You—startled me." I saw the movement of her throat muscles.

"I was just looking around," I said. "I'm sorry."

"Don't go," she said quickly. "Please don't go, Pete."

"Maybe it would be better if I did."

"No—I wanted somebody to talk to. I can't sleep. It's useless, trying to sleep. Please, Pete—a cigarette?"

I took a pack from my shirt pocket, shook one free for her. I lit it for her.

"Thanks, Pete." She turned toward the windows again, her cheeks flattening as she drew on the cigarette. There were tired lines under her eyes. "I've lived through another day," she said with a tone of wonder. "Now I have to face another. Tell me, Pete, was it that way with you? Did you hate to see another day coming?"

"Usually." My voice was rough with a sympathy I couldn't conceal.

"I slept this morning," she said. "Two whole hours. That's really…a triumph, you know. The rest of the day, I sat and let my nerves fight it out. I wondered what it would be like to kill myself. I wondered if I would feel any regret, in that last tenth part of a second."

"How long has this been going on?"

"About four years. It didn't come all at once. It was like a slow tightening. Days when I didn't feel quite right. Then one day it seemed as if I was hit by a big fist. Some of the nerves came loose. There's one now, twisting down my side until I think I'll go crazy."

She put a hand to her side, her face lined as if she were going to cry. She stretched out her arms, fingers against the metal slats of the Venetian blinds. Her breasts heaved fretfully beneath their frail covering.

"I've thought about it, Pete," she said. "I've had little to do but think about why, why, why I should be like this."

The cigarette wasn't doing anything for her any more. She turned from the windows to put it in an ashtray, then came back.

"Charley loved me," she said softly. "Once. Charley had a brilliant mind. He still does. But there's something inside him. Something obscene. He takes pleasure in knowing the wrong kind of men, sharing their secrets. We drifted into this kind of life. He stuck fast to it, gave up a good-paying job. It's too late for him to go back now. All the good is gone now. I smell the evil that seeps through his skin from associating with people like...Macy Barr. There isn't any way for me to get away. I think he'd kill me if I tried now. Devotion turned to possession; tenderness to lust. It was when I began to realize this that the fist began to pound me."

"I'm sorry," I said inadequately.

"Pete," she said with a dry sob, "I can't even cry any more. I'm just a crazy cardboard cutout of a woman. I loathe the man I can't get away from. The people who live around me sicken my stomach. My nerves torture me, all the time." Her mouth was petulant. She put her hands flat against her stomach, smoothed the nightgown close to her skin, pressing the hands as far as her rounded thighs. "I haven't slept with him in months and months. The thought of him touching me makes me retch." She was whispering now. "I've tried others. They...handled me as though I were a common streetwalker. It was no good—no good at all."

She reached out and took my hand, laid it against her side. "Can't you feel it? It twists and turns and jumps—they're knots and coils, tight and squirming—" She let go of my hand. She took the nightgown in both hands, twisted it, tore it, an expression of anguish on her glistening face. The gown was ripped, it hung away from her slim body. She fell against me, kissing me anywhere her lips touched my flesh. Her cheeks were hot and wet. "Make them still," she said urgently. "Give me rest, Pete. You can do it. Do it—do it."

I should have forced her away then but I hesitated an instant, and when the instant had passed it was too late. She was keyed to the point of hysteria. I was afraid of what might happen if I left her then.

"It won't be an answer," I whispered as I put her on the bed. "For a little while, maybe. That's all." Then I couldn't say any more. She moaned once and held me tightly, tightly, with all her strength.

When I left her, she was sleeping. Even in sleep the tenseness hadn't left her features. I wished I could help her. But there was nothing I could do. It was a lonely struggle. She would be the only winner, or the only loser.

I went downstairs and walked toward my room. Beyond the French doors I saw a man standing on the patio. From the size of him I knew it must be Taggart. He stood there without moving for half a minute, smoking slowly. Then he dropped the cigarette, walked down the terrace toward the bay.

I opened the doors and stepped outside. Taggart had reached the sand. I could see him against the sheen of moonlight on the water. He walked along at the edge of the tide, his head turned toward the bay as if he were searching for something. He carried a large towel over one arm.

When he passed from sight around a bend in the

island, I walked away from the house toward a growth of trees that covered the northern tip of the island. Most of the tangle of scrub had been cleared from among the palms, and hardy grass matted the rocky ridge of land almost to the slap of the waves.

Through the bent shadowy trunks with their saw-toothed thatching I picked up Taggart again. This time he wasn't alone. In a sheltered cove he extended the towel to a naked, dripping Diane. Her hair was silver in the moonlight, the lift of her arm liquid. Taggart didn't take his eyes off her as she dried herself, turning to cape the towel across her back, lifting one foot and then the other to the grasp of it. When she had finished she spread the towel on the wind-decked sand, lay down on it.

Taggart turned his head to follow her movements as she laid down on the towel. His hands came up unhurriedly and he unbuttoned his shirt, took it off, folded it and put it beside the towel. Then he unbuckled his pants, stepped out of them. When he had finished undressing he lowered himself to her.

I was about to trudge back to the house when I noticed a movement behind one of the trees not more than ten yards from where Taggart and the blonde Diane embraced. It was a man, shifting his weight very slowly to obtain a better view, taking care not to be heard. I put a hand on the square butt of the .38, then relaxed. The observer had turned his body just enough for me to recognize him. It was Owen Barr. I strained my eyes toward the tree behind which he had concealed himself, but I couldn't see him any more.

I was a little surprised at the eagerness with which Diane was receiving the huge, slow-witted gunman. I had a feeling this was only a repetition of other meetings between them. Then I grinned a bit wryly, realizing it didn't make much difference, and went back to my room.

Once there I felt I could use a drink and walked to the living room, helped myself to a bottle of good Scotch from the bar there. I took that and a glass of ice with four fingers of soda back to the bedroom, propped myself up on the bed and had a long cold one in the dark.

I thought about the strange crew assembled in this house. They made my head hurt. Sleep poured down on me like an avalanche. Before I was buried in it there was a warm clear light shining through the murkiness of twisted, pulped lives. Elaine. I reached out to her, forgetting all the rest.

I don't know how long I slept. When I awakened I stared into darkness as if I hadn't been sleeping at all, just dozing. I listened to a ratlike scratching, located the source of the sound near the dresser. I thought I heard someone breathing. Without moving on the bed I took my .38 from the nearby table, transferred it to my left hand. I reached up and found the light switch, turned on the lamp.

Owen Barr lurched away from the dresser, turned to me with a foolish grin. He took his hand out of the top drawer but kept it pressed against the front of the dresser for support.

"Well," he said, his lips loose, his eyes feverishly jovial, "am I in the wrong room? Huh?"

"It would seem that way." I kept the automatic pointed at him.

He gestured stickily with his free hand, listed unsteadily. I wondered if he was as drunk as he was trying to make out.

"Well, 'scuse me," Owen said, sniffing wetly. He took a step forward, but had to return to his support. "Y'see, I was looking for whisky. I thought this was my room, 'r somethin'."

"Sure."

He pointed. "Y'got some whisky over there."

"Don't you think you've had enough?"

He blinked. Then he leered knowingly. "Never have enough whisky."

I put my fingers around the bottle, without looking away from him and heaved it suddenly in his direction. He caught it with surprising deftness.

"Well," he said, licking his lips. "Well, thanks."

"Suppose you could drink it someplace else?"

"Oh, sure," he said airily. He put both hands around the bottle and set a course for the door, pausing once to lean against the wall. Then he was gone and I heard him mumbling in the hall. The door to his room clicked shut.

I got up and looked into the hall. He was gone, all right. I shut my own door and looked at the drawer Owen had been fumbling through. There was nothing in it but the large envelope containing the newspaper clippings Macy had turned over to me. The envelope had been opened. A couple of the clippings were loose in the bottom of the drawer. I assembled all of them, counted. There were only three stories about the fire left. I wondered what Owen was going to do with the other one. But I didn't really care.

Chapter Nineteen

Clouds boiled in off the Atlantic early next morning and it rained until after lunch, then cleared off.

In the afternoon some of us, including Macy and Evelyn Rinke, put on suits and went swimming. Taggart, Diane, and Charley Rinke didn't participate. They sat together on the terrace and drank Planter's Punch and Salty Dogs. Diane's face was as bland as ever. She paid no attention to Taggart. Now and then he would look at her over his lifted glass, a hint of pleasure in his eyes. Rinke was sprawled on a chaise longue, as if his long hours in the hidden room in the garage had depleted him. The lines of his down-turned mouth were still sharp, though. He looked as if he played lightly and skillfully with thoughts. Like juggled steel splinters, they could be potentially dangerous if he wasn't careful with them. He seemed to be the sort of man who would be careful.

"I thought you liked swimming," I said to Diane, on my way to the beach.

"Too choppy now," she said with a disinterested smile. "I don't like the feel of salt water in my throat." She was wearing shorts and another of those colorful half-sleeve shirts, this one of lime green. I shook my head in answer to her offer of a drink, went on down to the beach.

Aimee had a pair of swim fins and a face mask and she and Macy were diving for shells about twenty feet from shore. For all his awkward weight, Macy was a good swimmer, but his lungs couldn't stand all the work. In a few minutes he had to come out to rest, his face looking fatigued. Aimee scooted through the water gracefully, slanting deep with a kick of the wedge-shaped fins.

Evelyn Rinke sat at the edge of the water, where her feet were covered at each small rise of wave. Her hair was combed and she had put on some lipstick.

I kneeled beside her. "Feeling all right today?"

She nodded. "Um-hmm. Reasonably. The sun feels good, doesn't it?"

"Have you been in the water yet?"

"No. It feels sort of cold. I don't know if I'd like it. I haven't been swimming in a long time. Most of the time I stay close to the house—"

I offered a hand to her. "Try it."

She smiled faintly. "Well—" Her hard fingers closed about my hand. "All right. I think I will." We went into the water together. She gasped in dismay. "Oh, Pete!"

"Plunge in. You'll get used to it." She splashed me as she put her arms together and dived down. I followed her. She swam uncertainly at first, then more strongly. Aimee treaded water nearby, watching us.

"Not so bad, is it?" I said, gliding up to Evelyn. She smiled broadly, her face streaming. "It's awfully cold," she said, "but I like it." She lunged toward me suddenly, reached out and pushed my head under. I went deeper in the pale green water, grasped her ankles, tugged her toward the bottom. Her hair waved loosely behind her, a bubble or two escaping from her lips. She made a grab for me but I twisted out of the way. She went above water for air.

"Not fair," she complained, laughing. "I'm not used to

the exercise." She floated on her back for a few minutes, eyes closed, face relaxed.

Aimee's head bobbed up close by. She lifted the face mask. "Want to look for seashells?" she said timidly. So we looked for seashells. After a while Evelyn joined us. We crawled along close to the bottom, fingers searching the sand until it became impossible to see and we had to surface and wait for the water to clear. Once Aimee saw a small fish and sprinted after it, turning quickly in the water as she tried to duplicate the delicate fin-flip of the silvered fish.

We had been in the water about an hour when Macy bellowed, "Aimee! Diane says you better come in now." We all went in. Evelyn walked closed beside me as we waded ashore, bumping against me when her feet slipped on the uneven sand bottom. Then she stopped and held my wrist so I would have to stop too.

"Pete," she said, "I really had fun. For the first time in a long time. I didn't know anything could be fun any more."

I smiled at her. "Give yourself a chance once in a while."

She shuddered, putting her arms across her breasts. There was a stiff breeze and it was chilly after coming out of the water. "Here?" she said, looking toward the house, where her husband loafed on the chaise longue. A little of the old pain seemed to be returning to her. "Anyway, for a little while it was nice. Thanks, Pete. I guess I'll try to get a nap now." She walked on a few steps, feet splashing in the shallow water. Then she turned and looked at me again, not saying anything. I caught up with her and we walked to the house together, past the drinking set on the patio.

It was a quarter of five when I had showered and dressed. I was hungry and since I wouldn't be around for dinner I went into the kitchen and one of the boys fixed a steak from the freezer for me. After I had eaten I went upstairs, hoping to find Macy in his room. He wasn't there. I started down the hall, then stopped, hearing a peculiar sound from the Rinkes's bedroom. I waited for it to be repeated, then walked closer to the opened door. It had sounded like a voiceless person trying to scream.

I heard Rinke talking softly as I approached. While he talked the sound went on, relentlessly. I looked through the space between the door and frame. The first thing I saw was Evelyn Rinke's face. It was chalky. She sat as if her bones were glass. Her eyes were squinted almost shut. Her mouth was twisted open, frozen in the scream that was like a sawing of metal from her throat.

Charley Rinke was holding a cigarette lighter about four inches from her face. He moved it very slowly as he spoke to her in his low calm voice. Her eyes watched the flame, blank with fright.

"I know you're afraid of it, Evelyn," he said smoothly. "I'll take it away in just a moment. I know how you feel about being burned. This time I won't burn you. But I want you to understand this. Stay away from Pete Mallory. Hear me? I saw the two of you playing in the water today. You have a good time with him, don't you? But stay away from him. I know what you're building up to with Mallory. Just remember who you are. You're Mrs. Rinke. You're my wife. You belong in my bed, not anybody else's you happen to take a shine to."

In a moment of explosive anger I wanted to walk into that I room, feel his face smash and spread under my fists. Evelyn Rinke put her hands up, holding them out in front of her in a gesture of supplication.

"Take…take…take…" she pleaded.

Rinke thumbed the top down on the lighter and the little torch of flame was gone. He started out so quickly I had time only to retreat and duck into the adjoining room. I heard him walk rapidly away and go down the hall.

Evelyn Rinke was seated in the same position, hands over her face, when I went into her bedroom. She must have heard me come in.

"Go away," she said. "Go away."

"It's me—Pete."

Without any apparent movement she began to fall sideways out of the chair. I caught her and lifted her to the bed.

"Why did he do that?" I said.

Her teeth were tightly clenched. "He…can't stand to see me have fun. Not with somebody else."

"Why are you so afraid of fire?"

Her eyes opened wide. "Fire?"

"You were almost paralyzed looking at that lighter."

"I don't know why. The flame just makes me freeze up. I've always been that way."

I looked at her for a few moments longer. The terror was still in her eyes. She touched one of my hands. "Stay with me, Pete."

"It would be better if I didn't," I said. "If he came back I might kill him."

I turned and walked from the room. I went downstairs, my chest tight and squeezed with anger. I walked out of the house, toward the trees that capped the north end of the island, not caring where I was going, just needing to walk until the dangerous edge of hatred for Charley Rinke had blunted.

The sun was fading behind long streaks of clouds in the west. In the grove of palms I found Diane sitting on a couple of thin pillows, her back against the thickened base of one of the trees. There was a book face down in her lap and she looked steadily across the milky bay.

I stopped near her, putting out a hand to the tree. She didn't say anything. She didn't look up.

"Where's Aimee?" I said, to jar her loose from her attitude of concentration.

"Lying down before dinner," Diane said without moving. "What's wrong, Pete?"

"Why would anything be wrong?"

"I could tell by the way you were walking. The quick way you breathe." She looked up then. "Are you going into town?"

"Soon."

Diane sighed. She got up from the pillows stiffly. "Too dark to read," she said. "I guess I'll go now." She looked toward the bay again. "It's really beautiful here. I like to come here and just sit. Get away from things that aren't so beautiful." She looked a bit wistful. "I guess it won't be long before we leave this house for good."

"What makes you think so?" I said.

"It's—just a feeling I have."

"What will you do then?"

"I'll go where Aimee goes, I suppose," she said carelessly. "It doesn't really matter."

"You like the kind of life you've got here?" I asked her. "You like the people you live with?"

She looked away, bent to pick up the pillows. "I think we are in rats' alley," she said almost inaudibly, "where the dead men lost their bones."

The odd line jostled memory, and I looked at her thoughtfully. "Where did you get that?"

She shrugged. "I've known it for years. I've always liked that poem, because he seemed to write it for me. I'm the girl who looks in the mirror and wonders what difference it made."

I wanted to hear her say more, but she was suddenly silent, as if she had revealed too much of the self that she usually kept carefully wrapped and put away from the curiosity of strangers.

I took the pillows from her, stacked them under my arm. We walked back to the house together, saying nothing. Her jaw was set, and there was a melancholy look in her eyes, as if she were reaching back to another time that had held more promise than now. At the patio I left her and went to the garage, picked out a car for the drive into town.

Chapter Twenty

At seven o'clock I placed the call. I listened to the drone as it rang for a long time at the other end. Then she answered. "Yes?"

"You told me to call," I said.

"Oh, yes. Do you know where Railroad Avenue is?"

"I can find it."

"Get in touch with a man called Harry Small at Nineteen Railroad Avenue."

"Why?"

"He raised Carla Kennedy," she said. "He knows where she is now." The connection was broken with a hollow click.

I wrote the address down, left the Coral Gardens Hotel. In the car I unfolded my city map and found Railroad Avenue. It was a two-block street that ran diagonally into the Seaboard's Moreland Yards, not far from the bay.

I found the street without much trouble. It was hardly wider than a driveway, lined with gray, tottering rooming houses, narrow brick buildings. I parked near the entrance to Railroad Avenue, beside a littered embankment next to the railroad property. A long diesel freight pounded by on the outside track as I got out of the Buick.

Number Nineteen was half a block from the glittering bands of tracks. I picked out the number lettered above the door in the light of a lamppost on the corner. It was a deserted store of some kind. The windows had been painted over, and there was a large rusted padlock on the door. It probably hadn't been opened in years. Somebody had scratched a ludicrous face in the scaly paint near the keyhole.

I wasn't amused. I had bought myself twenty bucks worth of nothing. I looked up and down the dark street. Lights burned here and there in the high windows, but there were no faces, no people to share the ledge of sidewalk with me. I walked past the store slowly, stopped. There was a crevice between two buildings, barely four feet wide. A dozen steps down this brick canyon a small yellow light glowed feebly, making long groping shadows. There was a door beneath the light.

I listened to the sound of boxcars clanking together in the freight yard, the deep chuff of an old locomotive. I walked down the alley, my feet rattling the trash. A furry shadow raced from a small paper box ahead of me, darted into blackness beyond the reach of the light.

No one answered my knock. I looked down at the brass doorknob. It gleamed dully. No rust. I touched it. My fingertip came away clean.

I put my hand around the knob, turned it slowly. The latch clicked, the door was free of the jamb. I pushed it open.

Inside, it was stifling. The one window was shut, shade pulled over it. The only light came from a battered metal table lamp in the center of the room. A man sat upright in a wheelchair beside the table. He was a short man with a bald head, powerful arm and shoulder muscles. His hands dangled at the spokes of the big wheels. He wore a

T shirt, gray pants, suspenders. His face was yellow and
dry, the eyes half open and slightly protruding. His parted
lips twisted convulsively. He leered at me. It was nothing
personal. He would leer at anybody who came through
that door, even the cops who would have found him sooner
or later, if I hadn't come first.

I walked closer to him, trying to smell death in the hot
room. But he hadn't been dead that long. I found out
what was holding him up so stiffly. A knife had been
thrust through the canvas back of the wheelchair, getting
him just to the side of the left shoulderblade. From the
size of the handle I judged it was a pretty large knife. The
blade was aimed slightly downward. It had probably got
the heart or one of the important arteries nearby. He
would be a big sack of blood. A little of it had run down
his T shirt in back, dried darkly.

It would have required a husky man to stab him like
that, through the thick muscles developed from years
of self-locomotion in the wheelchair. The tread on the
rubber-capped wheels was almost worn away.

A stock of up-to-date newspapers and magazines with
the front covers missing suggested he probably made his
living as a newsdealer. His room needed a good cleaning.
He didn't have enough shelf space for all his books. They
were piled on the windowsill, on the floor, under a bunk
bed. There was one on the table near the wheelchair,
opened at about the middle. I glanced at the cover. It was
a collection of poems by Robert Browning.

Next to the Browning reader was a telephone, and a
small notepad was stuck halfway under the base of the
phone. I pulled it out, looked through it. It wasn't new,

but there was only one notation in the little book, a Bay-view phone number. I picked up the receiver of the phone, dialed. There were six rings, then a sound as if someone had cut in.

"Stan's Restaurant," a female voice said cheerfully.

I hung up, looked at the number again. I tore the page out of the notebook and shoved it back beneath the telephone. Apparently Harry Small had had Stan's private phone number at the restaurant. They cut in from somewhere else when he didn't answer.

Listening to the echo of my own thoughts in the silent room was making me nervous. Perspiration soaked my face. For a moment I almost envied him his dry skin.

I walked around the table and my foot kicked a piece of broken porcelain. I looked down and saw a little glazed figure, a Napoleonic soldier standing stiffly at attention. His feet and rifle were broken and there was a long crack down his face to the white cross-chest cartridge belt. I wrapped him in my handkerchief, not taking time to look for the missing feet, and put the broken doll in my coat pocket.

It was almost impossible to find anything in the cluttered room, but I gave it a try, looking in the most likely places for pictures. I found none. No faded snapshots of little Carla Kennedy. No trace of the girl at all. And Harry Small was supposed to have raised her.

I was ready to go. I had stayed too long already. But I went to the phone and dialed another number, the number the old woman had given me. It rang again and again. I waited for her to answer, but she never came. I hung up and wiped the phone with a towel from the sink. I thought about turning off the light above the door and leaving through the alley that led to the rear of the building. But I was liable to blunder into more trouble if I didn't go out the way I had come. I left Harry Small, smearing the doorknob with the palm of my hand as I went out. As far as I could tell, no curious eyes tracked my progress down Railroad Avenue to where the Buick was parked.

Chapter Twenty-one

At a quarter after eight I parked the Buick in a metered rectangle on Kelvin Boulevard, walked half a block to Monessen. Down at the other end of the street, near the apartment house where Victor Clare had lived, children gathered under a streetlight. This end of Monessen was deserted.

There were no lights in the grim brick fortress of the used-furniture store. I cupped my hands against the glass plate in the door, looked inside. It took me a few seconds to notice the splinter of light between the curtains at the rear. I watched it, reached out with my fist and knocked loudly. Nothing happened. I knocked again. The light went out suddenly.

I thought about that. Then I turned and walked across the street, stood partially behind a leaning tree to see if anyone ventured out. I waited for what seemed a long time. I decided it wasn't worth it, but I stayed there anyway. Then I saw the tip of a cigarette glow in an alley next to the store. Nothing else. Just the cigarette to tell me I wasn't the only one who waited.

In another minute or two, the cigarette was flipped away, toward the sidewalk. I kept my eyes on that alley. I counted the steps he might be taking. Then there was a crack of misty pale light along the side of the furniture store as a door was opened. I thought I saw someone go inside, but I wasn't sure. It was quite a distance. The light vanished as the door was shut.

I yawned to lessen springlike tension, put a hand inside my coat to loosen the automatic that rode in the shoulder holster there. I crossed the street casually, my shoes popping the crisp little asphalt bubbles raised by the heat of the sun that day. Down at the other end of the street the children played in the circular glow from the streetlight. A voice chanted, "Ten…twenty…thirty…" and there was a quick scuffle as figures fled to favorite hiding places. Soon there would be the long moments of breathless search, a yelp of discovery, a frenzied dash to the circle of light. Home free.

I walked into the alley.

"Seventy…eighty…"

I pulled the heavy automatic from the holster, slid my fingertips along the smooth, faintly oily slide. I put my thumb on the rasp top of the hammer, eased it back. I walked very slowly. I lived a long time between each step. The noise of the children faded, belonging to another world beyond the mouth of the tar-black alley.

This was the world now. A world of silence where you shot fast and quick at a misstep, a fatally accidental sound ahead. Scrape of shoe against an unexpected break in the pavement. Tiny whispering of fabric against a brick wall.

I found the depression in the wall of brick where the door was. I stopped again. He might not have gone inside. Or there might be another one a dozen feet down the alley, waiting with a gun on the door, waiting for me to frame myself in the dusty light. If it was a shotgun it would tear me in half.

My fingers touched the knob of the door. It turned without any difficulty.

If someone were waiting for me, he'd be as nervous as I was, as tightly wound, looking for an excuse, any excuse, to blast away.

I put the automatic in the shoulder holster for a moment, peeled out of my coat. It would be a poor decoy. It might not work. But if it did, I had him like shooting pigeons in the park…That is, if anyone were waiting.

Holding the coat by the collar, I turned the knob all the way. I brought the automatic up in my other hand, steadying it against my stomach. I pulled the door open, flung the coat high into the entrance so that it flared open, sleeves flopping.

Nothing happened. The coat landed inside with a muted plop. I went through the doorway quickly, rolled past the jamb and against the wall inside. Light came from a single unshaded bulb hanging on a frayed cord from the ceiling. There was no one here, either. There were many crates inside, pieces of broken furniture. Enough dust to shovel out.

And freshly made footprints in the dust on the floor. About a size-nine shoe. Not a very big guy. The tracks stopped at another door across from me. This door was open about two inches and there was more light in the room beyond. And voices.

I eased the alley door shut, picked up my coat and put it on.

I followed his steps to the other door. Only one person was talking. He spoke with a soft drawl. He talked almost incessantly, and there were overtones by a woman. She didn't speak. She moaned in terror and pain. The speaker didn't seem to mind this. He talked on. I moved very close to the door and stopped. I could see inside. It was the room where the woman modeled her figures. The fan was still on. I could hear it, above the frightened sobbing, the tough persuasive drawl.

The drawl went like this:

"Mothah, did you tell him wheah Cahla Kennedy is? Did you, mothah?"

"He…went to Harry Small. Harry…told…"

"No, mothah. Harry Small didn't tell him nothin'. He couldn't, because Harry Small is dead."

I couldn't tell where the man was standing in the room. The soft flowing voice was confusing, and acoustics were bad. It was Winkie Gilmer, of course. It had to be Winkie Gilmer. I felt very grateful that it was Winkie Gilmer.

"I want to know what you told him, mothah. Befo' I open up that othah cheek fo' you."

I kicked the door wide open and stepped into the room, knowing instantly that I had been suckered good, that Winkie Gilmer had been expecting me, had led me on with the drawling voice as he waited for me to come inside. I knew he was very close to me even as something chopped down on my wrist and the automatic jumped out of my hand. I felt as if I had grabbed a live wire. I did the only thing I could. I fell away from the direction of the blow and part of my flaring coat was ripped cleanly and noiselessly by the slicing blade.

I didn't go down but was wedged awkwardly between an old dresser and a defeated easy chair. I got my eyes on Gilmer then. He recovered with cat-quickness, brought the blade lower with a flourish, moved in on me with a little crouching step. I had to watch the blade. It was honed sharp, thin, about six inches long. Everything was happening in split seconds. I knew the futility of trying to squirm loose from the grip of the furniture. I kicked up and out hard, trying to get his elbow with the toe of my shoe. It missed, skidded off his forearm, but knocked the arm up and threw him off stride for a second. I sprawled backwards, my shoulders against the floor, head tilted against the wall, legs sticking up and out, one of them bent over an arm of the sagging easy chair. I couldn't have been more helpless.

But Gilmer had to wait another second, indecision in his eyes, before he could decide to lean across the chair, elude my legs and start the blade low, away from my arms, ripping out bowels and intestines and lungs with one jerking slash. It gave me a second to twist sideways, get one arm under the chair, one behind it, and throw all the muscles of my arms and shoulders into play as I lifted the chair, shoving it forward enough so that it tipped over into him just as he lunged, hitting him right above the knees. I followed the chair, shoving it like a football blocking sled, and Gilmer was carried forward a few feet, his body sprawled out.

Chair and Gilmer slammed into a shelf, and little modeled figures showered down. Gilmer had powerful legs. He was sitting on his rump at the base of the shelf but he kicked up, tearing the clumsy chair from my grasp, knocking it away from both of us. He scrambled up, his face reddening, his fist still holding tight to the knife. He was a stocky little fellow with a face like a college cheerleader. A pleasant-looking little man who wanted to slash my gut inside out.

I was just a little off balance. The human body is always off balance, unless you're standing still with both feet planted. The ancient Tibetan monks who worked up the sciences of jiu-jitsu and bar-jitsu knew that. There are ways to fight a knife flashing at you, edge up. The bar-jitsu boys make it look easy. Two slaps with either hand. A nerve bitten at the base of the thumb, on the back of the hand. The knife jumps away, there is only a pain in the forearm. It was something to know. I wished I knew. I only knew to duck low, under the knife he held at belly level, shoving forward to knock him off balance so he couldn't get the knife around and use it against my neck. I pushed him back and straightened up, taking my arms from around him, shoving his good right arm high so that he had to reverse it to make use of the blade. I got hold of the arm first and, when Gilmer's reflexes stiffened it, used the arm like a lever to throw him halfway across the room. He sailed in a flat arc to the table where the woman had worked at her figures. He hit the table on his back and rebounded slightly so that when momentum carried him to the edge of the table he was almost sitting up. He went off the table and sprawled face first into another shelf of figures. He got one arm up to ease the impact. The little dolls jumped from the shelves, popping against the concrete floor.

Winkie spun away. He wasn't holding the knife. His other arm, the one that wasn't in front of his face, lashed out and cleared a shelf of bottles. He would have fallen but his fingers gripped the edge of the shelf, and he held himself up. A broken jug of something that looked like linseed oil was emptying down over his face and the front of his shirt. He turned, one hand closing on the neck of the broken bottle as I hopped across the table after him. I was going to go into him with my fists but changed my mind in mid-air and hit him with both feet together, right above the belt. The broken bottle went spinning. Winkie's legs shot out from under him. His hands broke his fall.

Gilmer crawled to his knees. I had hit the floor after kicking him, and one of my elbows was numb. I was afraid it was broken. I turned on the floor to defend myself if he came after me. It would be a poor job with one arm. But Gilmer apparently didn't know I was hurt. He looked away from me quickly, his face wrinkling with alarm. I glanced under the table and saw the woman on her hands and knees near the door, picking up my automatic. I hadn't paid any attention to her until now. I saw blood dripping slowly from her face. The gun was all set to go off—when she found something to shoot at.

Winkie's eyes settled on a window. He went for it, picking up a chair along the way. In the time it took me to get on my feet he smashed out the window and went through it, feet first.

I followed him without bothering to retrieve my gun. He was a fleet shadow running through back yards a hundred feet from me. A fence in his way gave me a chance to narrow the distance. He looked behind him. He didn't have a knife, didn't have a gun. I was bigger than he was. Gilmer must have been unhappy. He ran the length of the fence, stumbled into an alley. He ran hard, waving his arms, legs working furiously. I ran more smoothly, with long strides, not using so much energy. Fear pushed him on. He stayed thirty paces ahead of me. Fences kept him in the alley.

Gilmer angled across the first street that intersected

the alley, heading for the square skeleton of a four-story building under construction. There were stacks of concrete blocks and lumber lying around. I sprinted harder, closing in on him. He stumbled, struggled across a mound of sawdust. I avoided the pile. His flight carried him inside the building. The supports and floors had been poured, and three of the ground-floor walls were blocked in. Winkie stopped, seeing he had trapped himself, then went up a ladder to the second floor. There were no stairs yet. I followed him. I heard him breathing hoarsely above me. He was only three rungs ahead of me.

He didn't stop on the second floor but continued upward. There was no place for him to hide on the third floor, either. Both of us were tiring, our speed of climb slowing. My lungs were bound with hot wires. We hit the last ladder. Winkie slipped once, hung by his hands. I came close enough to reach out for his foot. He pulled the leg up, scrambled up the remaining rungs. He was making shrill sounds of anxiety now.

On the top floor his hands found a length of pipe as he crawled away from the ladder opening. I saw him turn with it as I pulled myself up. There was flickering light somewhere and I saw the happy look in his eyes as he swung around, lifted the piece of pipe high.

"Now you gonna get it," he breathed. I got my knees over the edge of the opening, put an arm up. The blow knocked me flat on my back. If the pipe had connected with my forearm, the bone would have been shattered. Bunched muscles in my upper arm caught the blow. He lunged after me, intent on smashing my head with the pipe. I rolled quickly. There was an oily smell close by. I saw Gilmer hovering above me, his face and hair covered with sweat and linseed oil. It dripped off his chin. Sawdust clung to the oil.

My groping hand found the source of the smoke and the flickering light. My fingers scratched at hardening concrete. I kept my eyes on Winkie. The pipe was swinging backward. He was being careful to nail my head, alert for any evasive movement. I picked up the round flaming pot of kerosene that had been left to warn prowlers away from the drying patch of cement, flung it at him with a sweeping movement of my arm. I aimed for his chest. The little black pot bounced away, but the lick of flame had touched the linseed oil-soaked clothing and a bright flaring torch framed Winkie's surprised face for just a second before the fist of flame closed around it and charred the stubble of hair on his head, seared the flesh, blinded him. He screamed. His hands let go the pipe and he clawed at his burning face. He stumbled back three steps, shrieking wildly as the flames ate away all expression, staining the air with the scorch of flesh.

Then, surprisingly, Winkie was gone. I crawled to the edge of the rectangular opening in the floor where the stairs would eventually go, and saw him hit the sand floor four stories below. He landed on his back. The fire on his chest and head flared brighter for an instant, then steadily and quietly burned away his clothing.

There was a little pile of sand close by. I shoveled some of it into the opening with my hands and it hissed downward to shower over the burning body. After enough of it had fallen the flames were extinguished.

I went down the ladders with great care, every muscle trembling. I had to stop and rest on every floor. On the ground floor I glanced quickly at the gunman. Half of him was charred. The fall had probably killed him any-way. The stench was nauseating. I felt a touch of regret that he was dead. Now there would be no answers for my questions.

I got out of there, walked back to the furniture store through the alley, climbed in through the shattered win-dow. I stopped with one foot inside. She was sitting at the table, holding the gun in both fat hands. There was a maniacal look in her eyes. Her once carefully waved hair stuck out all over her head. Each breath she took sounded like a retch. There was a long gash on one of her cheeks, cutting deep through the fat to the solid cheekbone. Blood from it was smeared on her face and hands.

"Easy," I said, not moving. I couldn't be sure she knew me.

"Where is he?" she said in a hard voice.

"Back there." I nodded over one shoulder.

"You killed him?"

"He's dead."

Her fingers unclenched and the gun thudded on the table. I brought my other leg through the window.

"You see what he did to me," she said. "Oh, the dirty bastard. He cut me. He didn't need to do that. He didn't have to."

"You want a doctor?"

"Yes. Yes."

"In a minute you can have a doctor. First you talk to me. Where's Carla Kennedy?"

She fumbled for a handkerchief in her pocket, applied it gently to the cut. The bleeding had almost stopped. "I told you. I told you where to find her."

"All I found was Harry Small. Dead. Somebody knifed

him, somebody who probably knew him, or somebody he was expecting. I looked around his place. There wasn't any trace of the girl."

"Then—she took everything away."

"You don't know where I could find her?"

"No. I told you."

"This Gilmer. What did he say to you?"

"He wanted…to know what I told you. How did he find out I said anything to you?"

"I'm afraid quite a few people knew I was here. Did Gilmer talk or act like he'd killed Harry Small?"

"No. He just said Harry was dead."

"What did this Harry Small do for a living?"

"Newsstand. Up on Rosamorada, near the Strip. Used to sell papers on a corner downtown. Got his newsstand a couple of years ago."

"Do you know anything at all about Carla Kennedy that would help me? I've got to find her."

"I don't know anything. I just knew Harry took her in. I don't even know what she looks like."

I remembered something in my coat pocket, took it out. The little soldier was busted to a fair-thee-well now inside the folds of handkerchief. I unwrapped the pieces, scattered them before her eyes. She touched them fondly. One of her children had come home.

"I found it in Harry Small's room."

"It's one of mine." She looked up at me. "I made two of them, though. Just alike."

"Two? What happened to the other one?"

"Harry had both." I thought back, trying to remember another little figure in the room. Unless it had been hidden for some reason, there wasn't one.

"The girl must have the other one," she said, reading my eyes. She groaned. "Please. Call me a doctor."

"All right. Look. There's going to be Law all over this neighborhood when they find Gilmer's body. Questions asked. People will remember us running through their yards, through the alley. The cops will want to know about that busted window, how you got that cut on your cheek. It would be better if you don't tell them anything. There's another one like Gilmer around, only worse. He's killed quite a few people. He'll kill you just for associating with me, if you don't keep quiet."

The quick terror that flashed in her eyes gave me my answer. I went toward a phone on the wall near the curtains. My foot kicked something. I bent down and picked up a sky blue hat with a white band. I sailed it at the table.

"You better burn this in your kiln, too," I said. I made two phone calls, the first to the police, to tell them about Harry Small. The second was to a doctor whose name she gave me.

Chapter Twenty-two

Reavis was working the gatehouse when I drove back to the island. He came up to the car as soon as I was through the gate.

"We got company," he said, putting a hand on the window frame. "Maxine and three of his outfit. Also that girl he shacks up with."

I nodded, drove on up the hill. Maxine's car, a gleaming black Lincoln, was in the way so I couldn't get into the garage. I left the Buick in the drive, started to go inside.

"Mallory," a voice said. I turned from the door and waited. Charley Rinke hurried across the front lawn to me.

"They're here," he whispered, when he thought he was close enough.

"I know it," I said shortly.

He smoked nervously. "Mallory—Pete, this is our chance. The big chance for both of us. Macy is through. But the organization hasn't completely deteriorated yet. All that's necessary is for somebody to step in and take control. Two men could do it. You and I. I know the books. You've got the contacts. You could round up the men. In a few days we could smash any resistance. There wouldn't be much, if Maxine was dead."

I turned away from him. His hand caught my arm.

"Wait. Wait, Pete." His voice was strained. "Listen to me. I've worked it all out. We can do it. Think about it, Pete. You saw the money in the safe. There're millions more, just waiting for us to step in and take them."

"Let go of me," I said.

His hand dropped away. "What's the matter? I—I thought—"

"I don't know what you thought," I told him. "I don't know what kind of plans you made. But you better forget 'em, Rinke. You haven't got any idea what you'd be starting. With Maxine dead and Macy out of control this territory would be wide open. Every out-of-work Syndicate hood from Seattle to Newark would be down here on the first train. I couldn't hold this area with a battalion of Marines. It takes time to hire good men. You can't use any two-bit leadslinger who has a gun and is willing to work. You got to have some smart heads under you to try a play like that. Meanwhile your life wouldn't be safe from one second to the next. I don't know why I'm standing here explaining this to you. I ought to let you go ahead and try to take Maxine on your own. If you have the guts. I don't think you do. Your bright idea is for me to pick up the lead while you scratch around in the account books and sit back and enjoy the idea of being the local crime king. You wouldn't live a week. And when you died you'd die messy and scared."

He stared at me, his thin lips apart. There was an expression of childlike frustration on his face.

"I've got some advice for you," I said. "As soon as Maxine takes over you pack your tail up and get out of here. Go as far away as you can. Maybe change your name. You know too much to be hanging around town after Maxine is top man. He might get nervous about you after a while and tell somebody to chill you. Why don't you get an honest job somewhere and give your wife a break for a change?" It exhausted me, saying so much to him.

He sneered at me. "I can handle Evelyn all right," he said.

"I've noticed," I said. "Get away from me, Rinke, before I just sort of lean over and pound the hell out of you. It would probably do you good."

Rinke backed away from me hastily. "I thought you were smart. I thought I could talk to you."

"You can't talk to me," I said. "You don't have any words that interest me. All I'm interested in right now is getting a thousand miles away from this place."

I moved toward him and shoved him, hard. He almost fell. He backed away from me again. I didn't have to do that. There was no reason for me to do that. I turned away and walked into the house, wearily. I held my hands a little out in front of me as if I had smeared them with something dirty. I was tired of myself, of trying to be tough. I wasn't tough. I wasn't one of the hired apes who could smash somebody's face or put a bullet in somebody without feeling a twinge. I was conditioned to toughness, that's all. I was used to sudden violence and I knew how to take care of myself. But once in a while the guard came down and I started shaking. The only really tough men are the hefty lads with the sixty-plus IQ's who don't have the reasoning abilities of a flea, who can't see it happening to them someday. Who don't give a damn anyway.

In the brightly lighted living room, Gerry sat all by herself at the small curved bar sipping some kind of pale blockbuster from a tall etched glass. She wore a gray skirt and full-sleeved blouse with wide red stripes. Her skin was fresh as poured cream. She looked very young and very charming.

"Hello," she said, edging sideways on the bar stool, her lips pursed around a straw. "What happened to you?"

I glanced down at my clothes. I looked as though I had just been dug out of a cave-in. My hands were trembling. One palm was scraped. The arm that had been slugged with a pipe ached. I had trouble lifting it more than a few inches. I took out a handkerchief and put it to my face. It came away streaked with dirt. Mallory, home from the wars to count his medals.

"What are you drinking?" I said. "Ginger ale?"

"Don't be silly. It's some kind of rum thing. Stan showed me how to fix it. Do you want me to fix one for you?"

"Don't bother. One swallow would lay me out like a mortician's helper." I sat down in a chair of curved tubed aluminum. "Where's the gang?"

"They're all somewhere else talking business," Gerry said. "At least, Stan and Macy are." She drank the rest of the rum thing and put the glass up. "You haven't seen Owen around, have you?"

"Honey, I just got here." I had a thought. The tired wheels notched together as they turned. "Maybe you shouldn't see Owen while you're here," I said patiently. "You wouldn't want trouble to start, would you?"

She giggled. She reached for a square bottle of rum nearby, sniffed at it, dropped some over the ice in her glass. The giggle was a hint that she and the rum had been companions a bit too long.

"No, I wouldn't start any trouble," she said. "I used to live here. You didn't know that, did you? Macy used to think a lot of me, before that kid came along." For an instant there was a trace of bitterness in her eyes. "Good old Macy," she said ironically. Gerry turned slightly on the stool. "Even if I went to see Owen," she said, "Stan wouldn't send me away. He's always telling me that he can't live without me."

I sat there trying to work up enough energy to leave the chair.

She smacked her lips over the rum. "Not," she said mysteriously, "that he's going to live long anyway."

"Huh?"

She giggled again. "Shouldn't tell you." A stray bit of hair swooped across her forehead, giving her a roguish look. She smiled, the glass at her lips. Her teeth clinked against it.

"What shouldn't you tell me?"

She shrugged indifferently. "Oh. That Stan goes to the doctor all the time. Sometimes he goes three times a week. He should have an operation but I think he's afraid to. He takes these pills. Phen—pheno—"

"Phenobarbital?"

"I guess that's it. Some nights he lies awake in bed and groans." She put her lips against the glass again, kissing it. The flesh of her underlip looked soft and hot. She was a potent piece. I could understand some of Stan's attachment to her.

"It gets to be terrible," she said moodily. "I can't sleep."

Her eyes were dreamily thoughtful. "I think," she said, "that some night I'm not going to be there when he comes home."

I looked at her. "You mean you'd walk out on him?"

"That's right." Her head bobbed enthusiastically. "Leave. Time for Gerry to move on. There's this man I met. He's a count or something like that. I met him once when Stan took me to Boca Raton. He's very nice. He wanted me to come with him then. But I told him I'd have to think about it."

She put the glass down with a flourish, slid off the stool. She stretched, rising to her toes. The skirt fitted the curve of her legs. "Now I've thought about it," she said lazily, giving me a sidelong look. She kicked her shoes off. "Don't you think I'm pretty?"

"You're a darling," I said. "Queen of the junior prom. All the beanie-wearers are mad for you."

"That's not funny," she said.

I turned my head. "No, it isn't, is it? I'll have to go work up new gags. I think I'll take a hot bath while I'm at it. I think I'll run the water to the top of my upper lip and then make little waves. It should take me a long time to drown like that, shouldn't it?"

She looked at me solemnly, then her lower lip dropped and she laughed. "You're crazy," she said.

I got out of the chair. "Around here," I said, "that's a virtue." I walked out of the living room toward my room in the back wing. On the way I saw three of Maxine's boys playing poker in the television room. The Irish boy was one of them. He looked as if he were wearing an eggplant under his nose.

I stuck my head in the door. "Well," I said, "if it isn't Bushy, Bagot, and Green. And how is the king tonight?" Three jaws dropped. The one who was dealing threw a card wild and it fluttered to the floor.

"Gi da hell ow uh here," Irish said through stiff lips. His jaw looked sore. I went down the hall to my room, dragging my feet as if I had a tombstone tied to my back.

Chapter Twenty-three

I had taken a long bath and worked on my sore arm with some kind of rubbing compound and was about to get into bed when the door was nudged open behind me. I looked over one shoulder. There was a face in the doorway, about four feet from the floor. Serious brown eyes studied me.

"Hello, Aimee," I said.

The door inched open a little more. She was wearing blue pajamas and slippers with fur tops. Her straight black hair was brushed until it gleamed.

"I was lookin' for Diane," she said timorously.

"What makes you think she'd be here?" I asked her.

Aimee shrugged and crept into the room, her eyes peering around. Maybe she was lonely. She stopped at the foot of the bed and looked at me.

"Diane's not upstairs, is that it?"

She shook her head. "No. She went out when she thought I was 'sleep."

"But you weren't."

"No." She turned around and lifted her bottom to the edge of the bed, sat there, her hands folded. "She went to the garage."

"How would you know?"

She looked at me secretively. " 'Cause I followed her."

"What did she want in the garage?"

Aimee shook her head again. "She didn't go in." She scratched at her nose, thinking about it. "She went to one of those cars. A black one. She took a package out of it."

"A package? What kind of package?"

She held her hands about a foot apart, showing me. "Like this. I didn't pay much attention. I went back upstairs and went to bed before Diane came back."

"Then she went to bed, too," I said encouragingly.

"No. She got her swimmin' suit and put it on. She went downstairs in her swimmin' suit with the package. I think it was a box or somethin'."

"How long ago was that?"

Aimee shook her head. "I don't know." She sat very quietly then, hands folded, not looking at me. I glanced at my watch. It was twenty after twelve.

"Do you have a girlfriend?" Aimee said suddenly.

"Yes."

Aimee sighed. "If you didn't have a girlfriend, you could marry Diane, couldn't you?"

I frowned inconspicuously. "Well—not quite—"

"Diane should marry somebody," Aimee said worriedly. "Don't you like her?"

"In a way," I said.

"I guess Diane could marry Daddy," Aimee said. "But she don't—doesn't want to. Sometimes I think she doesn't like Daddy." She put her legs up on the bed and crossed them. "Diane's pretty," she said coaxingly. "I know she likes you, too. She said so. And she's not really as bad as she acts. I don't think so, anyway."

"You mean when she acts funny sometimes."

"No. Diane doesn't act funny. I mean not crazy. I'm talkin' about—" Her eyes seemed to become flat, suddenly blank. "But she said I couldn't ever say anything about that."

"About what?"

But Aimee wasn't talking. Her lips pressed tightly together. "Not ever," she said resolutely.

"Okay," I said. "Don't you think you ought to go back to your own room?"

"I don't want to if Diane isn't there."

"If she just went for a swim she'll be in before long. You could get into bed and leave the light on for her."

Aimee's eyes shied about the room. "Could I stay here a little while?"

"It wouldn't be a good idea. I was just going to bed myself."

Aimee hesitated a few moments, then slid off the bed.

"I'll walk you upstairs," I said. I took her hand and we went upstairs together. I thought about Aimee. When she was with me in the room, there had been the softest touch of something reaching out from her, a gentle tendril searching for an anchoring place. There was something very fragile about her, obscurely appealing.

In her room she got primly into bed and thanked me. Then she said, "I didn't bring teddy."

"What?"

"My teddy," she said with sleepy patience. "I must have dropped him downstairs in the hall."

"I'll get it," I said. I went back downstairs and searched until I found the stuffed animal. I picked it up and returned to the room. As I entered I saw that the bathroom light was on and the door open. Aimee was asleep.

Diane appeared suddenly in the doorway of the bath, drying her breasts with a towel. When she saw me she froze momentarily. Then she said, "Pete?" I couldn't see the expression in her eyes.

"Yeah," I said drily. I couldn't take my eyes off her. She was even better than I had imagined that first night on the beach. And with the bathroom light behind her there was nothing I couldn't see.

She watched me silently for a moment, making no effort to conceal herself with the towel.

"Why don't you come closer?" she said. She released the towel and kicked it away with one foot. She hadn't moved, continued to face me squarely.

I walked toward her, tossing the teddy bear on her bed. I could see her eyes glistening now, the gleam of teeth behind parted lips.

As I reached out for her she switched off the light behind her, leaving us in darkness. Her hands caught my wrists, pulling me to her. She made love to me with lips, tongue, hard-tipped breasts, movements of her thighs, driving me to the verge of insanity. When she took her lips away from mine I tasted blood. There was a pressure inside me that had my ears ringing.

"All right," I said, thickly, "let's finish it."

"It is finished," she said almost dreamily. "That's all, Pete. You can go now." She released me and stepped back, shutting and locking the bathroom door before I got to her.

I said something under my breath, wanted to put my shoulder against the door and drag her out of there. But I remembered the sleeping child, and the nasty little scene Diane had made with Owen Barr. I took a deep breath and went back to my room. It was a long time before I could get to sleep.

Chapter Twenty-four

The drinking started early next day, and by two o'clock the patio was jammed with those taking after-lunch refreshment. When I came outside Owen Barr was hitting the stuff hard, or so it seemed. Maxine drank nothing. He lounged in the sun in a pair of plaid shorts, wearing the most pleasant expression he had in stock. Things were going smoothly for Stan. The first conference had evidently cleared the way. There would be other conferences with lawyers on each side, some outside help from the hierarchy. But Stan was on his way.

Gerry sat beside him, wearing a fetching bit of swim suit that wouldn't have bandaged a sore thumb. She did Stan's drinking for him and they held hands. Owen Barr kept away from her, but now and then looked bitterly in Maxine's direction. When his glass was empty he held it out negligently and a houseboy would whisk it away and reinforce the ice with a jolt.

Charley Rinke and his wife played Canasta at a little table under a canopy of pink umbrella. Neither showed any interest in the game. Their fingers sorted the cards mechanically. Evelyn Rinke wore a big pair of sunglasses that masked any expression, but her complexion was sickly.

On the little dock that stuck out into the bay, Aimee, Diane and Macy waited while Rudy gassed up a sleek new speedboat. Rudy was wearing swimming trunks and seemed chipper, though he still limped painfully. Macy held tight to Aimee's hand, probably not pleased at the prospect of bumping along the bay in the speedboat. Aimee was bundled in an orange lifejacket.

There was little conversation, either on the patio or on the dock. Even Aimee seemed to feel the undercurrent of tension, and chattered very little.

I shook my head at a tray of highballs offered by one of the help and walked toward the terrace. Taggart leaned against the rock wall surrounding the patio, wearing shorts and a T shirt over an impressive display of muscles. He glanced at me for a long moment when I went by.

On the patio behind me somebody lurched out of one of the chairs so that it skidded metallically on the paving. I looked back. Owen Barr closed in on me, grinning drunkenly. He had a half empty glass in one hand.

"Mal'ry," he said slurringly. "Ol' Pete Mal'ry. Ain't you goin' to have a drink, buddy?" He put a heavy arm around my shoulders as he caught up to me, leaned against me so I had to stop or let him fall.

"Here," he said, extending the glass he held. "Y'take mine. Y'have my li'l drinky, Pete, an' I'll get another one." He spoke loudly, breathing in my face. There wasn't much of an alcoholic smell. I frowned.

He leaned his reddened face toward my ear, turned his face toward the bay. "I'll be so terrible *off*-fended if you don't have one drink with me, buddy." In another voice, low and quiet, he said urgently, "I've got to talk to you, Pete. Later. I can't say any more. I'm being watched. Come to my room." He burst into rasping drunken laughter.

I pushed him away from me. "Watch what you're doing," I said. "You spilled some on me. Get the hell out of here. If I want a drink I'll go get one."

He looked injured. He stood holding the glass in a tilted position in the palm of his hand, and his mouth sagged foolishly. I looked quickly at the people on the patio. No one was paying any attention to us.

"Well, I was—jus' tryin' to be helpful. Tha's all I was doin', Pete." He shrugged and weaved back to the patio, slumped in a chair, looked at nobody. I went on down to the dock.

Rudy had capped the big red gas can and set it on the dock. He climbed into the driver's seat now, started the motor. Aimee jiggled on one foot and then the other, impatient to go. Diane watched without interest.

The motor missed a couple of times. Rudy kneaded the accelerator. The flesh on his white back trembled loosely as he turned the wheel experimentally. The motor idled. He looked back over his shoulder at us.

"Better let me run it out into the bay and get the kinks out," he said to Macy. "She hasn't been used for a long time." Macy waved him away. He seemed preoccupied. Aimee looked up at him unhappily but said nothing.

Diane glanced at Macy. He told her to let go the lines.

"You might as well ride along," she said.

"I'll wait till Rudy loosens it up," Macy said. "Untie him."

Diane kneeled and freed the rope, tossed it into the stern of the speedboat. Rudy eased away from the dock, upping speed gradually.

"I'll swing around and pick you all up in a minute," he yelled back over his shoulder. The front of the speedboat bucked out of the water, kicked spray high. Two hundred feet from the dock Rudy began to lop. As he did so the gleaming speedboat blew apart without warning. There was a flat booming noise, a geyser of water mixed with splinters of the hull and the roll of dirty smoke. It happened with the quickness of a magician's sleight-of-hand trick. While the pieces of boat rained into the water and the echo of the blast rolled across the bay we were shocked still. I thought I saw Rudy hurled from the wreckage but I wasn't sure. I watched the boil of soapy foam at the spot where the boat had exploded. Then I went into the water, diving off the dock, seeing in passing the shocked sick face of Diane, hearing Aimee's open-mouthed cry as she realized something had gone wrong but wasn't quite sure how bad it was.

I came up swimming hard toward the debris bobbing in the ruffled water. I had little hope of finding Rudy but I didn't think about it. I tried to save as much strength as I could for the return trip, but I swam badly, hampered by my stiff sore arm. Every stroke made the arm ache fiercely. I didn't look up until I brushed past a piece of the boat skin. Then I stopped swimming and treaded water, searching for some sign of Rudy. Twenty yards out I caught a glimpse of his head, then his back as he rolled to the surface, hung motionless for an instant in the swell. His lungs must have been almost full of air when he went into the water.

I struck out quickly, dived when I reached the approximate spot where I had seen him. Ten feet down in the murky water I caught an arm and hauled him up, my lungs weighted and burning. I didn't pause to see what kind of shape he was in. I put a hand under his chin, towed the bloated leaden body. I couldn't see well. Salt stung my eyes. I sighted the dock, swam toward it. I went very slowly. The fingers that gripped Rudy's chin were sticky with something. I didn't dare waste time and strength looking at him.

When I thought I was going to have to let him go to save myself, a head bobbed up in front of me, a muscular arm reached for Rudy. It was Taggart.

"I'll take him," he said. I released the burden of Rudy gratefully, went for the dock with slow slapping strokes, my arm muscles trembling. My breath came in little flutters. Hands reached down at the dock to help me from the water. I lay on my back on the rough flooring, chest heaving, muscles jumping in my legs. I was too exhausted to move a finger. Dimly I heard shouted orders. Somebody told the women to get away from there. Somebody else said in an awed voice, "Jesus, will you look at *that?*" There was a muffled series of tired curses. I rolled over on my stomach, still gasping.

They were pulling Rudy over the edge of the dock— what was left of him. His mangled, mashed body had washed clean of blood. One arm and part of his head were gone. I saw ribs gleam from a gaping tear in his side, the armless side. The blast had got him along the right side of his body. I looked away from it, sat up on the dock. I glanced down at my hand, the one that had towed Rudy. There were clots of red between the fingers. I washed the hand hurriedly in the bay, leaning over the edge of the dock.

It was oddly quiet now. There were six men on the dock. Nobody said anything. Taggart sat with his arms around his legs, his face against his knees. He breathed explosively. The wet T shirt clung to him, showed the tanned skin underneath. There were specks of red on his T shirt.

I stood up, hoping my legs would hold me, staggered a step to remain upright. I saw the women clustered on the patio, looking at us. One of them—it seemed to be Evelyn Rinke—held Aimee in her arms.

Macy stood near the ruined body of Rudy—the last one, the last of the old gang. His shoulders were bunched. His fingers flexed like snakes maneuvering to strike. He looked at Rudy for a long time, his face frozen. His head edged up and he looked out at the bay. Then he turned on stiff awkward legs. He looked at each of us with bleak angry eyes.

"I was supposed to be in that boat, wasn't I?" he said. His voice was little more than a frightened hiss. "Me and Aimee." A sudden breeze fluttered his hair. There was dead silence for a moment. Macy raised an arm suddenly, threateningly.

"Get out!" he screamed. His voice was a slow curling lash that probably could be heard on the patio. "I want everybody out of here. Quick! Get off this island! Pack and get out!" His whole body shook from the force of his rage. Charley Rinke shuffled his feet nervously. Maxine's men looked at Stan questioningly. Stan nodded his head toward the house, his mouth grim. From a quick look at him I thought that Rudy's sudden death had shaken him as much as anyone. They edged off the dock, plodded toward the house. Owen Barr followed, tottering in the sand.

Taggart got up from where he had been sitting. His

face betrayed no shock. "What do we do with him?" he said, speaking of Rudy.

"Bury him," Macy said. "You and Pete and Reavis. Bury him. Then you get out too." Macy shoved by us and walked off the dock, his eyes watery from grief that may or may not have had something to do with Rudy.

He hurried up the beach and terrace with thick-bodied haste. The little group of men and women on the patio scattered to let him through. He gestured violently at them. From far away, almost as if it came from a place behind the sun, I heard Aimee's high cat wail.

Chapter Twenty-five

Reavis brought an old tarpaulin and two shovels from the garage, dumped them on the dock. There was a faint tremor in his lips as he looked at Rudy. The body didn't bother him. He had seen bodies before. But he had always left them for someone else to bury.

Taggart and I folded the tarp once, laid it flat beside the corpse, rolled him onto it. We carried Rudy in the sling, Taggart going first, staggering a little in the sand. Reavis followed with the shovels. Occasionally they clanked together. The sun was gone and the sky was graying.

In the cove where I had seen Diane and Taggart two nights before, we put the tarp down and began to dig a dozen feet above high-tide line, at the base of a rocky spine of land. There was some wind now and fronds shook in the trees with a dry rustle. Nobody said anything. The only other sound was the chuff of shovels as we dug into loose sandy ground.

When we had a rough rectangular hole about four feet deep we stopped. Any deeper and it might begin to fill with water. We turned to the lumpy tarp and swung it into the new grave. I made sure the covering was tucked around Rudy's remains. It seemed a small courtesy. Taggart leaned on his shovel and watched with flinty narrowed eyes. Reavis ran a hand through his hair and seemed anxious to leave.

"It don't make any difference to him whether he's covered or not," Taggart said. "Let's shovel him under and get out of here."

"Ain't we goin' to say anything?" Reavis said.

Taggart turned his head. "Like what?"

"I don't know. You usually say something when you bury somebody. I don't know what you say. I ain't no preacher."

Taggart's lips crooked. "He ain't no preacher," he said to me in a dry humorless voice. "You got any words that might save his soul?"

"If he ever had one," I said, "I suppose he used it as a down payment on a bottle of whisky a long time ago."

Taggart looked again at Reavis. "You got anything to say, go ahead."

"I ain't got nothin' to say," Reavis mumbled, as if he were embarrassed for having brought it up.

Taggart straightened. "Well, I have," he said. He took up a shovel of dirt, rained it onto the canvas with a turn of his wrist. "So long, Rudy. You must have known it would happen to you some day." He turned and flipped the shovel at Reavis. "You help Mallory cover him up. I'm goin' back to the house."

"You leavin' right away?" Reavis said.

"No. Not right away. I'll hang around a while."

"Soon's I get packed I'm goin'," Reavis said. "There's plenty of cars."

"Don't take the blue one parked by the gatehouse," Taggart said as he walked up the slight slope. "That's mine." I watched him stride through the trees and disappear over the rise toward the house.

Reavis stepped forward with his shovel, dug it almost

viciously into the pile of dirt. We worked hard for another five minutes, shoveling and scraping the fill over Rudy's body, making a long mound. When we were through we looked at each other, then turned and walked away from the grave site.

"I'm glad I'm gettin' out of here," Reavis said. He looked sideways at me. "Somebody had to wire that boat," he said, as if he had received a sudden vision.

"I know it."

"I don't want to hang around where I could maybe get it by accident," he said.

When we reached the house Reavis walked on down to the gatehouse to pack. I saw Stan's boys loading the trunk of his car with large boxes that might have held the files from the room in the garage. Maxine was dressed in a creamy-brown suit and his hair was combed neatly. He stood by the car with a snappy smile, supervising the loading process. When the trunk lid was closed he put out a hand to the door, glanced at the house. In another month he would probably have that, too. Gerry sat in the front seat and kept looking at him as if she were impatient to get rolling.

I couldn't let Stan go without saying goodbye. I walked toward the low black Lincoln and called to him. His boys had wedged themselves into the back seat and Stan had the door on his side open. He turned to me and the smile changed a little bit and became a confident smirk.

"I guess you heard," he said. "I've taken over now."

"Congratulations," I said. Gerry was staring at me from inside the car and I waved casually to her. "How's the Count?" I asked her. She averted her face carefully.

I put out a hand to Maxine. He reached for it, but I slid the hand past his, tapped him in the stomach. He faded back against the car, bending a little, a warning of pain in his face. His poise cracked some.

"Have you asked the doctor how much longer you're going to last?" I asked him.

He glared at me.

"Or are you afraid to?" I said.

"Get away from me," he said venomously.

I gave him a big fresh warm smile. "All right, Stan," I said. "But you better watch yourself from now on. You're in big business now. You know how it is. There's always some little guy who thinks he might like the fit of your shoes."

He gulped and tomato-color brightened his cheeks. He took a step toward me, then turned and jumped into the car, slammed the door. It shut with the finality of a lowered coffin lid. I thought about Rudy and Stan. Stan would have something a little more fancy than a paint-spattered tarp. He would roll slowly on hushed black tires to a place of gently waved lawn. But at the end of the journey there would be just another hole, as Rudy got—as everybody got. No matter how far it was to the graveyard, everybody got the same once the trip was over.

The wheels grabbed and screeched as Stan gave it too much gas. Then the Lincoln moved forward smoothly, away from the house.

Behind me another motor started. I looked at the car as it went by. Charley Rinke drove slowly after Stan, slowly enough so that I could see the touch of smile at a corner of his mouth, the satisfied tilt of his head. I had an idea that Rinke had made an eleventh-hour connection and his life wouldn't be altered too much because of Macy's departure. His car followed Maxine's obediently through the gate.

Mrs. Rinke sat beside her husband. I wasn't able to see her face. She had her hands over it, tightly, as if she planned to keep them there for a long time, as if she were afraid to peer out at the world and the nightmare shapes that had sprung up in it.

The wind was stiffening now, coming around the north corner of the island and frothing the surface of the bay. There was nothing soft and gentle about the wind. It matched the color of the sky, and it was teething. I felt it harsh against my face.

Reavis had come out of the gatehouse with a suitcase. There were two cars parked off the road just outside the gate and he walked toward one of them, after closing the gate from force of habit. No need to shut the gate any more. Nobody would want in now. Turn off the juice in the fence. In a week it would be overgrown with creeping things.

I turned and walked toward the house. In my room I put together my few things and stored them in a suitcase one of the houseboys had dug out of a closet. They were getting ready to leave, too. Macy had paid them off. They seemed happy to be leaving, preparing for the long march to the highway where they would catch a bus.

I was about to toss the shoulder holster and automatic into the suitcase too, then changed my mind and put it on. I couldn't be sure, but I might not be through with it yet.

Macy came in while I was checking all the drawers to see that I had everything. He looked as sloppy as he had the night I had arrived. He had dressed hurriedly, and missed a buttonhole in his haste. One side of the shirt was higher than the other. He lugged a big suitcase with him and parked it just inside the door.

"I called the airport," he said, almost panting. "Plane's waiting for me. No time to do this right. We were going by boat first. We'll fly down to the Caribbean now. There's an airstrip that isn't watched on an island I know. Stay with me until I'm on the plane, will you Pete?" There was a note of pleading in his voice. Fear was icing his bones. The .45 was stuck into a big hip pocket of the grape-blue slacks he wore.

"I'll drive you," I said. "What have you got in the suitcase? You unload the safe?"

He nodded nervously. "I took close to half a million. The rest can stay there for now."

"Who's going with you?"

"Diane and Aimee. They got passports and everything. They're fixed up legal. I'm not. It don't make any difference." He looked back over one shoulder. "Everybody gone?"

"Maxine and his crowd pulled out a little while ago. So did the Rinkes. I saw Reavis leave, too."

"Watch the suitcase for me, will you, Pete? I'm going upstairs, pack a few things. Diane and Aimee are getting ready to leave. We'll lock the house up and get out of here."

He turned and hurried out before I could say anything to him. I glanced at the suitcase, then put my own beside it. A sudden gust of wind rattled the window. It was darkening outside. There would be a storm before long.

I walked out into the hall, hearing the French doors banging. I shut them, secured the latch. Outside, the palm trees shuddered and dropped in the grasp of the wind like witches shouting incantations. From somewhere close by I thought I heard a thump that I couldn't identify.

The door to Owen Barr's bedroom was open. I remembered that he had been lost in the sudden frightened shuffle after the speedboat explosion. The last time I had seen him he had been plodding toward the patio after offering me a drink I didn't want.

After...

I walked into the bedroom quickly, remembering the cold steadiness of his voice as he had talked urgently to me. Something about being watched. Maybe he imagined it. But maybe there was a good reason for his anxiety.

He wasn't in the bedroom. Some of the paintings had been taken from the walls, stacked on the bed. It was the only sign that the occupant might have considered moving out.

There was another thump. This time I got it. It came from the bathroom. It might have been a shoe hitting the side of the bathtub.

I pushed the bathroom door open, stepped inside. Owen Barr was lying half in the tub, half out of it. I saw the curve of his back over the side of the tub, and the protruding ridged handle of a switchblade knife. His foot moved just a little against the side of the tub, and there was the thumping sound again. It was getting weaker every time. I leaned over the tub and put my hand on his shoulder. I could see half his face. Blood ran out of his mouth and into the drain, a tiny red river in a white wasteland. His eyes were half open and had the look of a chloroformed frog. I thought his lower lip was twitching just a little.

"Who did it?" I said. "Who knifed you, Owen?" Maybe it was too late. Maybe the speech mechanism was rusted shut. But he tried to talk, and I could sense the great effort, though his face didn't change much.

It was a tiny gurgling whisper. "Didn't see…" That wasn't all. He had more to tell me. One of his fingers curled a little. I didn't dare move him from the awkward position.

"Carla…Kennedy. I saw her. Back was burned. Watch out, Pete…"

I put my face closer to his. "Who is Carla Kennedy, Owen?"

I don't know if he heard me. He was a few seconds away from dying and what was in his mind pressed hard to get into words.

"She got…box from…car…threw it in…bay…I got it. Hid…hid in…bot…"

The last word stuck and he never finished it. He died quietly, with one last tiny shiver of breath. The blood spilling from his mouth had a metallic gleam.

I got up slowly, holding the few words that had come from him as if they were something light and delicate that would disintegrate and be gone forever if I wasn't careful. There was a warning sound in my brain but I was too intent on something else to listen to it. Owen had hidden the contents of the box. I went into the bedroom, already beginning to suspect the answer I would find, but needing to know.

The bedroom was no different from all the others. I took the closet first, searched hurriedly. No place of concealment there. I turned to the dresser. The top drawer was jammed full of expensive underwear, socks, various accessories. I scooped them out of the drawer, pitched them toward the bed. Underneath I found six wrapped quarts of whisky lying side by side like bombs in an arsenal.

I scooted them out of the way one by one, stopped. One of the packaged bottles was far lighter, and there was no shift of liquid in it when I picked it up. I tore the sack away from the bottle. The top had been broken off once, then clumsily reglued. I took the neck and shoulder of the bottle and rebroke it with my hands. The contents of the bottle spilled into the drawer.

I looked at the items. Two neat clippings about the fire that had burned to death the family of Carla Kennedy more than twenty years ago. A little model of a Napoleonic soldier, trim and erect, rifle on his shoulder, coat a bright splash of red. A child's locket, engraved *Carla from Pop.* It was an old locket, blackened in places. My fingers searched through snapshots, some of them old and yellowed. A family portrait. Another picture of a girl about thirteen, standing beside a man in a wheelchair. The most recent picture showed the invalid man, older now, beside a sidewalk newsstand. He was smiling proudly. He was all by himself. The newsstand was hung with gay streamers. It was opening day. Carla was probably there. But that time she wouldn't want to be photographed. She wouldn't want anyone, except maybe Stan Maxine, to know of her connection with the crippled news dealer in the wheelchair.

I had found Carla Kennedy. Like a lot of things you find in life, she had been found too late.

"Turn around, Mallory," I heard a hard slow voice say.

Chapter Twenty-six

I felt the brush of a bony hand across the nape of my neck. It was too late to think about being careful now. I turned very slowly, holding the broken piece of bottle.

Taggart was all dressed up and ready for town. He wore a new blue suit and a self-conscious little bow tie and there was a small revolver in one outsized hand. It pointed right at my stomach. His face had about as much expression as a beach pebble.

"Where is she?" I asked him. I wondered how close he was to pulling the trigger. It might come without warning, with no spreading of lips or crinkling of lines around the eyes. But maybe he had just enough dislike for me to wait and let the fact that he was going to kill me soak in. It was a hope.

His hard lips came apart an eighth of an inch in a sly smile.

"Who do you want?"

"You know who I want," I said. "Diane. Carla Kennedy. Which name do you know her by?"

He ignored that. His eyes caught the movement of broken glass in my hand. "Drop that," he said. I let it slip to the rug.

"She's down by the gatehouse," Taggart said. "With Aimee. Waiting for Macy to come looking for Aimee."

His big square feet moved a little uneasily, as if he

realized he was taking too much time with me. "She's going to kill him herself. I get to take care of you."

"Like you took care of the others?" My lips felt large and numb. It was an effort to talk. I began to feel the rise of fear, the kind that freezes you stiff. It was working up through my legs without haste. I was always conscious of the gun under my arm. But with Taggart's little revolver steady on my stomach, it might as well have been hanging in the closet—unloaded.

"That's right," Taggart said. He was getting a curious sort of enjoyment talking to me. It was even loosening up his face muscles some.

"You were the traveling boy," I said, trying to keep my voice smooth and level, with no sudden pauses to give away my panic. "You had the chance to run the old gang down one by one and cut their throats. Sooner or later you could make all the territory and nobody would get suspicious. Just old Taggart doing his job. You use the same knife that's sticking out of Owen's back?"

He didn't comment. He looked cool and efficient in the crisp blue suit. Some mother's boy had grown into this. He couldn't he quite sane.

"What about Harry Small? How did Diane feel when you bladed him? Or was it her idea?" Just keep talking, Mallory. Just keep jamming that thumbnail brain so he can't get down to work.

"Diane said we had to," he admitted. "She said you were going to find him and he'd talk about her. She didn't want to do it."

"But I was hard to kill, so she didn't have a choice. You tried twice. I suppose you were with Winkie when he pulled the shotgun ambush. It would be your idea. Did you doctor the Buick over on Monessen, too?"

"Yeah." He looked faintly puzzled. "How did you get out of that? Nobody saw me."

"Only a little boy who didn't look old enough to talk. He should grow up and get J. Edgar's job. He deserves it."

Something happened inside Taggart then. I could feel it happening. I could sense the ponderous slow thoughts swinging around to the problem at hand: my death.

"How did Diane talk you into this?" I said. "Those passionate midnight meetings on the beach. Did she tell you she loved you?"

He took a full step toward me, as if I had bitten a nerve. His mouth opened. "She does love me. I love her." He made a sad calf noise in his throat. "Did you ever see her back? She's beautiful. But her back—it's ugly. Macy Barr did that to her." The gun nosed up a little. "I love her. I'd do anything for her. Anything she asked me. We're going to go away together. Nobody ever loved me before. I never got anything but kicked around, because I was a bastard. Everybody hated me. They looked at me with hateful eyes and wished I'd run away. Diane doesn't hate me."

From outside the house, above the sound of the wind, there were two shots, sharp cracks spaced a second apart. And a child began to scream in terror, as if the shots had unlocked a hidden place inside her and old nightmares tumbled out, writhing in her mind.

Taggart thumbed back the hammer. I was going for the gun anyway. It was no good—my fingers would never touch it—but it was no good just to stand there and die, either. A second before I shoved my hand toward the butt of the .38 there was another shot, different from the first two. Heavier. The faraway roar of a .45. I knew Macy had somehow got to the automatic in his back pocket. Taggart knew it, too. He was thrown off stride by the sound of it. The slow-focusing mental processes were off me for a full second.

I had the gun out and shot him twice in the chest before he could do anything. The blows from the heavy .38 slugs would have knocked an ordinary man flat on his back, but he was not ordinary. Two more shots came together, blending in a hot stunning roar. One of them was his. I felt it hit like a pole thrust sharply, end first, into my stomach. I had tipped the barrel of the .38 up half an inch before the third shot. The first two set him up so that his head was turned slightly to one side. The third slug tore his throat out and went on into his head at an angle, along the jawline. He turned a little more, his eyes glazing, and then his legs failed and he pitched downward, spouting blood.

I backed away from the wreckage, feeling sick. I had to lean against the dresser. The automatic was almost too heavy for my hand but I continued to hold it. I knew the wound was bad without looking. I felt blood trickling down the inside of one leg.

I reached down and found the hole and put the heel of my hand against it. I walked with clown steps out of the room. I put my shoulder against the wall and slid along it, pushing grimly toward the living room. There wasn't so much pain. It was more the idea that I was hurt that frightened me. I felt a swooping dizziness. It would be better to sit down, but I had to get outside. If she was still alive I had to stop her. I remembered Aimee's shrill scream.

There was no more sound now, except the treacherous howl of the wind.

The front door was open. I put the fingers of my hand around the knob of the screen, but it was hard to turn because I was holding the gun, too. Finally I got it open, but I had leaned forward too much and fell outside with the swing of the door, rolling down the steps, feeling the blunt edges against my back and arms and shoulders. There was a pain in me, as though someone's hands were tearing at my gut.

I lifted my head, looked down the curved drive to the gatehouse. Thunder grumbled above. Swirling clouds pressed low upon the island.

Aimee was lying motionless on her back near the drive, arms spread, one knee up. Diane walked past the child slowly, not looking at her. She had a gun. She was watching Macy, who lay on his belly a dozen steps from the gatehouse. Macy didn't move. There was an object near him that might have been the .45.

Diane aimed carefully at Macy. In that same moment, he seemed to stir, an arm moving slightly. He wasn't dead yet. I raised my own gun, taking time only to see that I had the right direction. I had little hope of hitting her.

I squeezed off the remaining shots in the magazine, the big automatic jerking in my hand, the noise deafening me. Then a sudden spasm left me weak. My face was cold, my eyes full of perspiration. I let go the gun and wiped at them. It was odd that she hadn't returned the shots. I looked up again, hauling myself to my knees. For a long moment I could see with perfect clarity.

Diane had fallen near the gate. She must have panicked when I began to shoot, and tried to run. The gate seemed to be locked. She hooked her fingers over stiff strands of wire, pulled herself to her feet, leaned for a moment against the gate, as if she were trying to shove it open. There was a car parked on the other side, pointed toward the causeway.

Something was wrong with one of her ankles. She might have twisted it when she fell. She glanced up, then put her arms above her head and began to climb the woven wire gate laboriously. It was eight feet high. It would take her only a few seconds to wriggle over the top and reach the car on the other side.

I tried to get up, sat back groaning from the fury of sudden pain. All I could do was watch her. She seemed to be having some trouble. Then I became aware that someone else was watching her, too. Macy Barr.

His head was lifted no more than half an inch from the ground. He looked at her for a few seconds, then began to crawl forward. I saw where he was going. Not toward Diane but to the door of the gatehouse. Once he stopped, and I thought he was finished. But with an awkward lunge he reached his feet, staggered forward to the doorway, leaned inside.

Diane saw him. She had reached the top bar of the gate, was ready to lift one leg and then the other over the top, drop to the ground. But fear held her fast for the seconds she needed to jump to safety. She stared at Macy and there was terror in her eyes. Above the gathering shriek of the storm I could hear her own scream, lifting to meet the lashing wind that whipped at her hair.

"Don't, Macy! No—"

She was still screaming when Macy threw the switch inside the gatehouse that electrocuted her mercilessly while her tortured body jerked and wrenched in a useless effort to be free of the clinging current.

I put my head down and waited. I knew there would have to be a time when I would find enough strength to go down there. I waited patiently for that time and finally I got to my feet and shuffled through a dark tunnel of angry rain to the gatehouse, found Macy dead on the floor. I closed the switch. I walked past him and looked at a telephone. I picked up the receiver and with a finger as large and awkward as a banana I dialed a number that would bring help. Then I sat on the edge of the bed trying to hold on to slipping strength. The child would be wandering in the rain, lost and afraid—if she were still alive. I thought she might be. Diane wouldn't shoot her.

It was all over. But I had to wait with a hole in my stomach and wonder. Sometimes they could fix it, and sometimes they couldn't. I had bled only a little from the mouth, with all the walking around. That encouraged me. But still you never knew.

I hoped Elaine would be able to get to me fast. I wouldn't feel so afraid then.

Chapter Twenty-seven

First there was the hospital. Memories of it were sporadic, vivid, unorganized. Bits and pieces of colored glass in a clear jar. Moments of knifing pain. The upended bottle and long tube attached to one arm. An oxygen tent. A whirring circle of crisp clean whiteness. Faces, of course. Expressions of masked uncertainty, professional optimism.

And fear. Elaine was the one who was afraid. She held tight to one hand during the great swinging loops in and out of darkness, the bird-wing beat of pain in my stomach. Then the hand wasn't there and the faces were careful little masks until there wasn't anything but eyes peering at me and the measured drip of chloroform on a pad across my nose. I wasn't very interested in anything. I couldn't quite remember why I was there. It didn't seem to matter, except that I was probably sick. No, not sick. I remembered, then. Shot. Maybe it was bad. There was no time to worry about it. There was no time.

Afterwards I was bound tightly about the middle. They wouldn't let me eat. Tubes in the veins nourished me. Elaine's face was more cheerful. The faces that came with badges weren't. They were weary and irritable from overwork and trying hard to be polite but not really caring. Some of them were government badges. I told them everything I thought was safe for me to tell. I told it about nineteen times on successive days with a doctor standing by and after a while the badges went away with tired sighs. The papers printed very little, Elaine told me later.

I grew stronger. Lying in bed, I tried not to think. One of the badges—gold-filled—came back to see me, a well-dressed guy with a pink face. He talked to me for a long time, alone. Afterwards I was completely clear. He got mad at me three separate times because I wouldn't tell him everything he wanted to know. He tried to convince me I had enough information to wreck organized crime in the area. I told him it wouldn't stay wrecked six months, and meanwhile I'd have bought myself a hole in the head. He saw my point. He signed some kind of release and the hospital said I could go home. My doctor from Orange Bay came down, checked me over suspiciously and took me back in a red and black ambulance.

Two days later Elaine came into my room at the clinic with the morning newspaper.

"Good morning," she said. "How did we sleep last night?"

"Better," I yawned. "Still have that middle-of-the-night period. Wake up reaching for a gun that isn't there. Then lie awake as if I never have slept and never will again."

She took away the breakfast tray with the food I hadn't eaten and sat on the edge of the bed, her hands folded in her lap.

"You promised you'd finish telling me about it when you could," she said.

I sighed, put aside Steve Canyon and the other denizens of the comic strip page, and began the long story of hate and vengeance. I told her of the old fire and its lone survivor, the little orphan named Carla Kennedy who grew into a lovely woman carrying the terrible scars of the fire on her back and the even more terrible scars of hatred in her festering mind. I told it all, how she had used the dull-wilted giant, Taggart, as a messenger of death, how she had ruthlessly removed all obstacles to her crazy plan: the ineffectual drunk, Owen Barr; the crippled news-dealer who had been like a father to her; me, when I began to dig too close to the truth. Except that she had failed to get me, three times.

Elaine's face tightened when I told about Taggart's last, nearly successful try at me. Her fists clenched as I described the gunfight and my long, tortured trip to the outside, too late to do the job Macy had called me back to do.

I began to tell of Macy's last, long struggle to the gate-house and the death switch, but Elaine shut her eyes and put her hand on my lips. "That's enough," she said. "It's… terrible. I don't…ever want to hear you mention it again, Pete. Never. It's just a miracle you're alive. I want to forget all that ever happened."

I took her hand, kissed it. She looked at the door, then leaned back on the pillows with me. I put an arm around her shoulders. "As soon as I'm well enough to get away from here, we'll be married. Then we'll take a long trip. Havana or Nassau, maybe. It was nice of the cops to turn over that envelope they found in Macy's pocket to me, just because he had put my name on it. Five thousand dollars. We'll spend some of it because I think I earned it. The rest belongs to Aimee."

I felt Elaine stiffen slightly, but her eyes remained closed.

"How is she?" I said.

Elaine smiled bleakly. "She eats. She sleeps, a little. But she won't respond to me, or to anybody. She...just sits, and stares with those dark terrible eyes. Dr. Richman says she'll probably snap out of it."

"We'll do what we can," I said.

"Yes, Pete," she said obediently.

"You didn't like it when I had her brought here, did you?" I said after a short pause.

"Pete, we don't need to talk about it now."

"Come on," I said. "Let's clear it up."

She twisted a little, indecisively. "Pete—she doesn't belong with us, really. She...she'll never fit in. We know nothing about her, except that she's probably not legitimate. We know about the filth and squalor she came from. She was wild once. She could go back to being wild. She might grow up to be nothing but grief. A...busty, sullen little tramp, easy pickings for every boy in town. She's—trouble for us, Pete. Trouble we don't need to take on ourselves. We'll have children of our own to think about."

I tried to tell her the way I felt, but I knew I couldn't explain. Not now. It was something she would have to learn, and maybe she was right, and I was wrong. But I had to do it this way and because Elaine believed in me she would go along with it. Reluctantly. But she'd try.

"Maybe she'll turn out to be nothing but trouble for us," I said frankly. "But I think she deserves some sort of chance. Macy gave me more than a chance once. I—I don't quite know what to say."

She got up then. A smile warmed her eyes. She bent over and kissed my forehead. "It's all right, Pete. Really. We'll do the best we can. And it'll work out for us.

Just...be patient with me, darling. Understand me. I guess I was born a snob, that's all."

I held her for just a moment. "With you as a model, Aimee will turn out just about perfect." Her lips touched my face again; then she walked out quickly, snuffling and having some kind of trouble with her eyes. She slipped through the door, and it clicked softly behind her. I smiled once, then turned on my side, so the sun was warm on my face. I waited for her to come back.